Critical acclaim for Peter Cunningham

'*The Sea and the Silence* is a terrific novel. It is moving and hugely entertaining'
Roddy Doyle, Booker Prize winner

'Peter Cunningham is a writer of great gifts'
Barry Unsworth, Booker Prize winner

Tapes of the River Delta

'Cunningham is uncompromising in his commitment to the plain storytelling of old-fashioned romance and the effect is something like that of an old-fashioned movie that is apparently uncomplicated but yet becomes a classic'
John Kenny, *The Irish Times*

'Peter Cunningham writes beautifully; each character is expertly defined'
Caroline Clark, *Literary Review*

'[Cunningham] has remarkable powers of description, and his landscapes are breathtakingly visual, but he can also turn his hand to smaller, domestic detail, and there is a wonderful twitch of dry humour in his prose'
Stephanie Merritt, *Observer*

'Cunningham's prose combines the strengths of the traditional storyteller, which he must have learned in the days before such strengths became unfashionable, with the insight that can only come with maturity'
Graeme Woolaston, *Herald (Glasgow)*

'It is a long time since I have been so delighted and entranced by a book ... for those who care about fiction here is an unforgettable voice'
Madeleine Keane, *Sunday Independent*

'Clever ... brilliantly conceived ... Cunningham's descriptive writing is as superb as his characterisation'

Sue Leonard, Irish Examiner

Consequences of the Heart

'Cunningham, a magician with words, has penned a vast panorama of a novel. His set pieces trail a magnificence of grandeur, yet his prose can also glide effortlessly into the quivering recesses of the human heart'

Vincent Banville, *The Age (Melbourne)*

'Simply breathtakingly brilliant'

Kevin Myers, *The Irish Times*

'The intense passion of this book, like the nature of love it attempts to portray, is seductive, courageous and spellbinding'

Jim Clarke, *Sunday Independent*

'A joy to read'

Arminta Wallace, *The Irish Times*

'Sparkling prose ... great inventiveness ... powerful images that reveal a rare talent for descriptive writing'

Mike Milotte, *Tribune*

The Taoiseach

'Nobody should call a book a work of genius on a first reading, but at its best this one approaches genius'

James Downey, *Irish Independent*

'A powerful narrative'

Daire Dolan, *Irish Post*

THE SEA AND THE SILENCE

PETER CUNNINGHAM

**NEW
ISLAND**

The Sea and the Silence
First published 2008
by New Island
2 Brookside
Dundrum Road
Dublin 14

www.newisland.ie

ISBN 978-1-84840-005-4

British Library Cataloguing Data. A CIP catalogue record for this book is
available from the British Library.

Typeset by TypeIT, Dublin.
Printed in the UK by Athenaeum Press Ltd., Gateshead, Tyne & Wear

New Island received financial assistance from
The Arts Council (An Chomhairle Ealaíon), Dublin, Ireland.

10 9 8 7 6 5 4 3 2 1

IN GIRUM IMUS NOCTE ET
CONSUMIMUR IGNI

We go in circles by night and are consumed by fires

(Anonymous)

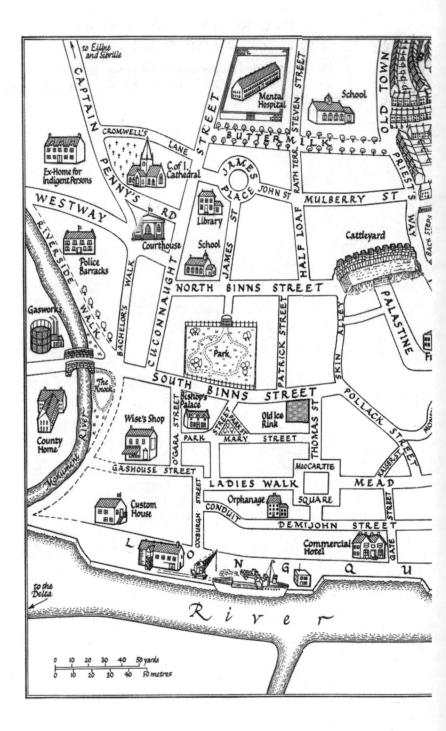

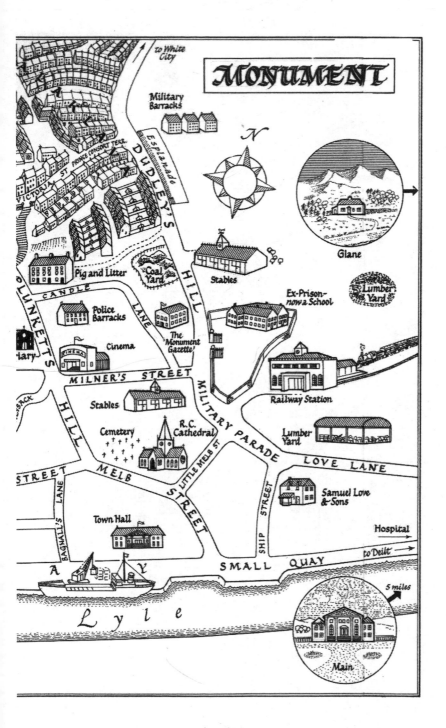

Carol

PROLOGUE

By ten in the morning, the fug from the river at low tide had already crept into the upstairs office in Mead Street. It is ever so in mid-August, thought Dick Coad as he closed the window. At almost any other time of year, he could discharge his daily quota of probate, insurance claims and conveyancing of property to a background of ships loading or discharging and the clanging of wharf cranes, but in August, when the tide was low, the River Lyle's gum-like, perspiring mud banks released a mephitis which oozed across Long Quay into the streets and up into the centre of the town.

On the desk before him lay an opened envelope and a will.

Dick reread the will, and for the second time that morning was overwhelmed by loss. Unmarried, childless, he nonetheless had much professional experience of both marriages and children, having presided over the sundering and distribution of each to a point where, had he been less wise, he might have felt that he understood them. She had been a caution to any such presumption. Although he had known her over many years, he had never been able to grasp why she had taken certain decisions. Beauty like hers, he would have once thought, made women free.

Neither had her appearance changed until near the end, and then it had been hard to watch. He had wept that day on the train home from Dublin, four months ago, for he had known it was over. Not that a solicitor could shed tears for every client about to die – many rejoiced – but she had been different. Dick would always see her as he had that first day on the platform in Monument Station: he was expecting a Mrs Shaw from Sibrille, and this beautiful young woman appeared.

Dick cracked a match alight for a cigarette and through a tail of smoke observed the distant river beyond the chimney pots. Her instructions were curious: for herself, cremation. Dick was to scatter her ashes on the sea at the point beyond the lighthouse where the tablet was set. He knew the spot well and was part of the committee responsible for the memorial's upkeep. Curious, but appropriate.

All her real property, including the house in Dublin, was bequeathed to Miss Bibs Toms, instructions that had caused Dick to smile four months ago, and now he smiled again.

Finally, he was to read the contents of the two taped-up parcels. Dick lifted them onto his desk. The first, in black letters done in a felt pen, said, '1: Hector'; the second, '2: Iz'. Miss Toms had told him on the telephone that the second parcel had been finished only six weeks ago.

Dick sliced open the wrapping paper with a paper knife.

His instructions were clear. He was to read the contents of these parcels. Then, he was to destroy them.

1
HECTOR

CHAPTER ONE

1945

I had heard so much about it that, like all things eagerly
awaited, I was prepared for disappointment.

— Are you ready? Ronnie Shaw asked, and I smiled.

— This better be good, I said.

We breasted a hill, pulled up and got out. The truth is, I
gasped. So much sea and, by comparison, so little land. As
I stared, by one of those miracles of light, the sea shone as
if all the silver of the world was buried just beneath its
surface.

— Well? Ronnie asked.

— It's beautiful.

— I knew it! he cried. — I knew you'd say that!

He caught me up by the waist and lifted me in the air.

— Ronnie!

— I see the sea! he shouted, whirling us round and
around.

We were both shrieking.

— Ronnie, you'll drop me!

— I see the sea! he cried as I clung to him and laughed for the pure joy of it. — I see the sea!

❧

Today it would seem odd – it would seem inexplicable – for a woman of twenty-three not to have seen in advance the house and place in which she was destined to live, but in Ireland then, petrol was severely rationed, trains ran irregularly and long trips were undertaken only in emergencies.

Ronnie's car, an MG Midget of the late 1930s, had squeaked and jarred throughout the six hours of our journey south, and as we came in along the quays of Monument, every surface gleamed and shined from recent rain, and rain squalls had buffed and energised the chessboard-like dairy country beyond Monument too so that it glistened through the full register of summer colours. As we turned off just short of the village and drove out along the causeway, the rain began again and the car's single wiper whipped back and forth with fierce determination.

The Shaws' sprawling home stood behind the old lighthouse in a garden of rioting hydrangeas. A wind-blasted croquet lawn with correct white hoops stood disdainfully on a small promontory. As we got out, a sudden screeching erupted above our heads as seagulls wheeled, light glinting on their bellies. Ronnie brought my hand to his cheek.

— Our lighthouse, he said with such pride that my

affection for him rose even further. — Is there something funny?

— It's the most wonderful lighthouse in the world! I laughed as we walked arm in arm along the causeway.

To our right, above high, yellow cliffs, cattle grazed. The rain rolled down in wet veils onto the gently toiling water so that between rain and sea there was no distinction. This was the sea I would relate to most during my early days in Sibrille, the way I first found it, for although it could rise into furies in which the lighthouse itself would be engulfed, or only the next morning lie still as a mirror, it spoke to me most during summer's days of warm, misty rain.

— Here's something I told you about but you didn't believe me either, Ronnie said and his eyes popped.

— Could I ever have doubted you in anything? I asked.

— Probably not, he said, his moustache twitching.

We had come to the end of the natural groyne where a rectangular tablet had been set, facing out. Four columns of names, more than a hundred in all, were recorded. They had been blown off course on their way home having fought the French and had met their watery end here, off this jagged point. Under their names, the inscription:

Their Lives Were Cut Short
By The Awful Dispensation Of An All-Wise
And Inscrutable Providence

☙❧

We had married in the Catholic church in Sutton, outside Dublin, with my mother, Violet, and Ronnie's parents, Langley and Peppy Shaw, in attendance. Then Ronnie and

I had driven north, across the border into County Down, and had spent our four-day honeymoon in an enormous hotel between the mountains and the sea.

The Shaws were in all but one respect a typical Anglo-Irish family, which, in 1945, meant people of some means and land for whom achievement meant nothing unless it related to a horse. But they were Catholics. Although religion ran quiet in Ronnie, it ran true. His father, Langley, had arrived at his majority with his inheritance in tatters: unsupervised land agents had diddled the books for twenty years. Lofty and lanky, eighteenth century of manner in his courtly, unconcerned way, with his perpetual smile and his refusal ever to be ruffled, Langley had been educated in England by Benedictines and had come home, and although his bankers had murmured their reservations, in 1890 had built an oratory in Gortbeg, their then-large estate, at a cost of £2,500.

By my time, over fifty years later, the old days were spoken of as a golden age, relived in well-practised anecdotes. A staff of eleven had been maintained inside and out, notorious among whom was the butler, Johnson, blighted by polio down one side, who had applied butter to the afternoon tea bread with his tongue.

Religion, on the face of it, was of little consequence in 1922 when a local militia came to burn Gortbeg. However, an advance warning had been sent enabling Langley to ship out furniture, paintings and chinaware, so although the burning honoured ancient rituals, the saboteurs were less than committed and only the east wing, which included a breakfast room with wallpaper by Pugin, was razed. Bureaucracy triumphed where fire had failed. More than a decade later, Gortbeg and all its lands were acquired by the new government and paid for in non-negotiable bonds. Langley went to London, disposed of a diamond the size of a wren's egg, put £2,000 into War Loan and bought the lighthouse, the coastguard station and fifty acres in Sibrille.

∂∾∾ᕗ

Ronnie amused me, and always had, from the first day I met him. What had once come across as pompousness, even arrogance, was in fact an utter belief in himself that was endearing and frequently comical. He had gone to Belfast in 1943 to join an armoured regiment and had taken part the following year in shoring-up operations in France, where he was lucky not to have been killed by a German sniper. Shipped back to hospital in England, he had spent the remainder of the war completing a correspondence course in estate agency, which enabled him when he came home to put letters after his name: Captain Ronald Shaw, MBVI.

— Ever tell you why I decided to join up?

We lay on the soft summer grasses of the cliff in late July. Ronnie's elbows jutted for the sky, their leather patches glistening. Between us and the horizon, I could see men in mackerel boats, working their lines.

— Was it because your father wanted you to?

— Absolutely not. The only thing my father approves of killing is foxes.

Ronnie had a gap between his two front teeth, which, along with his big eyes, made even his attempts at being serious amusing. He said,

— I was sitting out here, in this exact spot, one evening in 1941 and I could actually see German bombers blowing up cargo ships.

— From here?

— I could see the explosions.

— I don't believe you.

Ronnie looked up at the seagulls. — Would someone please explain to this beautiful woman that I am incapable of deception?

—Very well, I believe you.

— Thank you. Well, as I say, here I was and out there I could see this appalling behaviour. On our sea. I decided I just had to stop it.

I laughed. — And so you did!

Ronnie sat up and looked out to the horizon. All of a sudden he looked like someone marooned in time from another era. I said, — It must have been hard.

He put his arm around my shoulders. — I was lucky, he said quietly. — Many weren't.

— I know.

—We shall always pray for them.

We had both been brought up the Anglo-Irish way, where to show emotion was ever seen as weakness. Ronnie leaned out, plucked a sea-pink by its stem, held it up for a moment, then tossed it over the cliff.

—To absent friends, he said.

Without warning, I felt my breaths coming short.

— Ronnie …

— My God, I'm sorry, I've upset you.

— No, it's not that.

— It's not?

I turned my face away and closed my eyes.

Ronnie said, — Are you unwell, darling?

— Sort of, I said, turning back to him. His round eyes and startled face made me sniffle and giggle at the same time.

— Oh, God, what? he said.

— Ronnie, I think I may be pregnant.

☙❧

Langley and Peppy lived in the coastguard house, together with a woman called Delaney, Ronnie's nurse who now cooked, and, for most of the year, Peppy's younger brother, Stonely. One's first impression upon entering the coastguard house was that a burglary had taken place. Doors and the drawers of cupboards and chests stood open or pulled out in every room, and from the innards spewed their incoherent contents. On the floors stood mounds of books, sacks of potatoes, the wheels of bicycles, rubber boots, riding crops, stacks of pictures, golf clubs, boxes of cartridges, fishing rods, waders, suitcases, jam jars, cases of gin, propagating vegetables, milk churns, bedding, the mounted masks of famous vixens, oil drums, boxes containing the Gortbeg chandeliers, camp beds, step-ladders and a rocking horse. Such disorder went unnoticed by the inhabitants, who picked their way carefully through the chaos until they found what they sought – a book, or a cup for tea, or a chair without a cat on it.

When I first met Langley, he was stooped and arthritic, spindly legged and alarmingly thin, but the one time I saw him hefted up on a difficult mare of Peppy's, I grasped in an instant how he fitted his horse, the lightness of his hands and how all the soreness went out of him. He had hunted for more than fifty years with wily, ragged-tongued hounds, spreading them over the tricky gripes around Gortbeg like a tan cloak. Man and beast, earth and sky, human blood and river water became all the one to him. He had lived it not once, but countless times; once a week, Langley fell to his knees in the church in Sibrille and thanked God for His munificence.

༺ঔ৵৵

In the vast, upstairs room of a nursing home not far from Dublin's Shelbourne Hotel, my baby was born. The doctor stayed with me all night, and three nurses. With all my heart I believed that I was going to die. As they kept passing the cold flannel over my brow, I could feel the shape of my veins standing out there. Then, just when I had screamed my utmost and begged for death – for me and for my child and for the whole world – I could feel an easing in the bones of my pelvis, which must have dislocated. On my thighs, I felt the blood rush out onto the rubber sheets and then the most unforgettable feeling, the passing from me of such a warm and solid proof of my own happiness as it moved, still partly in me, and I reached out my wet hands, crying although I didn't care who knew, pumping blood, and I said, — My love.

Ronnie had been up two days before, lunching at his club, bemused by the fussing nurses. Telegrams were sent to Sibrille relaying the news, but I didn't expect to see anyone until the end of the week and so was surprised when the next day the door opened and Peppy walked in.

—You poor child, she said and kissed me, her nose cold as mutton. Many years before, her father had bought her a house in Dublin and she sometimes came up to inspect it. Now she went to the cot in the corner of the room. — Oh my God, he's big enough, she said, sniffing. — Just as well he didn't go full term.

Peppy's winters were given to fox hunting and shooting, her springs and summers to sea and river fishing.

— Is he taking his bottle well? she asked.

— I'm feeding him, I said.

Peppy frowned and sat in a wing-backed chair the nurse had brought over. — I never did.

— Could you not?

— Oh, I expect I could have, I can't remember, but they thought it better not to.

— The same here, but I insisted.

— If one must, then not beyond a few days. Peppy shivered, then smiled radiantly. — You look so beautiful!

— How is Ronnie?

— Delirious. He'll be up tomorrow, or Thursday. He's cub hunting.

I laughed.

— I told him to be careful, not to break his neck before he'd had a chance to see his son and heir, Peppy said. She glanced to the corner. — No causes for concern?

— They say he's perfection.

Peppy removed her hat and lit a cigarette. She bent forward and unlaced her leather knee boots and shook them off, then blowing smoke from the side of her mouth, sat back and crossed her legs. She said,

— I remember when Ronnie was born. I had him in Gortbeg, the most dreadful experience. Langley was in and out, but the person I missed most was my mother.

— You must have been lonely.

Peppy looked towards the windows. — Unimaginably.

A nurse came in, picked up the infant and brought him over to me.

15

— A little man like this'd be much better off with a big, big bottle, she said.

I said, — He's got two big, big bottles here, thank you, nurse.

Peppy watched the baby searching for my breast. She said,

— He's a Shaw for sure.

I smiled, but Peppy was pensive. — I wanted to get out of England, you see, whatever that took. Three of my brothers had already been killed in the Great War and Stonely was handicapped. Our home was like a nursery for death.

— Then you met Langley.

— I came over here to hunt, he followed me back. My father was too distracted to take much notice of him. We were married in a church outside Carlisle, following which Langley, drunk, rode in a point to point and had such a heavy fall that he subsequently never remembered anything about that day, including the wedding ceremony.

Tea was brought in and the nurse took the child from me and winded him. Peppy dropped a lump of sugar into her cup.

— After six months here, I made a rule that I would never ask, and I never did. Never 'Where were you last night?' or 'What were you doing?' Never. I took up fly fishing.

I felt for her, this bony, plain woman who had so much to give.

— Was it bad? I asked softly.

Peppy slurped tea, put the cup to one side. — I can't remember, to be honest.

— Were you never in love?

— Love is something I've never quite grasped, although I daresay you have, she said.

I closed my eyes.

— Yes, I said. — I have.

But Peppy became flustered now, for she thought that she had said the wrong thing.

— Oh, God, I am sorry, Iz. What I meant to say was that I was never as beautiful as you, and so I expect you know far more about love than I do – and that's not what I meant to say either.

— I understand.

— Do you? You see, some people never quite get the hang of it and I'm an example. I have other things, though, and I've never been one to sit and think of how it might have been. But come on, any more of this and we shall both be sniffling and there's nothing worse. Tell me, what are you calling it?

— His name is Hector, I said.

Chapter Two

1946

Where I had grown up, in the Meath countryside more than an hour's drive from Dublin, all our shopping had been done in the store of the nearby village. The Shaws, on the other hand, never shopped in Sibrille, but bought everything in Monument. Once a week, Ronnie drove me to town, where I handed in my grocery order at the counter of Wise's, the grocers, and then made my way up into the teeming section known as Balaklava where at the tiny, fly-blown premises of Shortcourse, the butchers, I ordered our meat.

In those first months, being in Monument pierced me, but, in time, she became as I had thought of her on my very first visit: a port that was more Mediterranean than Irish, not just because of the sense of relative plenty in an Ireland that was striving to survive on war rations, nor because of the exotic faces one encountered when ships

were in, but because Monument herself, in her architecture
of terraces and arched doorways, her labyrinthine streets,
lanes, courtyards and back steps and her almost Moorish
churches discovered behind an ancient palisade or beyond
a rusting portcullis might well have been forged in a distant
land and floated in one foggy morning from the sea.

❧

I made my way in with Hector by the never-locked back
door of our lighthouse and climbed the curving stone steps.
The child looked up at me and smiled in such a recognisable
way that, for a moment, I was swept away on a flash flood
of memory. Later, in the middle floor with its cheery
fireplace, I sat with Hector on my knee and beheld the
panorama laid out below. In Sibrille, we saw the sun down
all the way to the sea horizon, and every day the point at
which it plunged moved so that I could measure off its
progress on the windows of the lantern bay. The sea lay flat
when the wind was off the land, as it was that day, allowing
a glazed path of red to run all the way from the sun to the
lighthouse. I felt tired much of the time, which was not at
all unusual, I had been told, in the year that followed one's
first baby. I slept a lot and often when Ronnie was late, he
spent the night downstairs on the big sofa so as not to wake
me.

As we watched the sunset, I heard a car drive down the
causeway. It was a long, sleek maroon car with enormous
brass headlamps, I saw as I looked out. It pulled in before
the house and Ronnie got out and straightened his hair
with his hands and put his cap on. Because of the sun's
reflection on the car's windscreen, I could not see the

driver. Ronnie stooped forward, saying goodbye. I saw a woman's hand reach out, a thick, gold band at its wrist. Ronnie held the tips of the fingers briefly, then as the hand disappeared, he straightened up and turned around and looked directly up at me.

We lived, in the main, independently of his parents and, each evening, I prepared a meal and set a table in the lantern bay and we both sat down after gin and had dinner together.

— How is my family? he asked, throwing his cap on a chair. He leaned to kiss me, then Hector.

— We're well, thank you.

I watched as he poured us drinks, his steady hand, the long, reassuring curve of his back in its tweed jacket. There was no tonic to be had then, so we took our gin with water and a tiny drop from an old jar of bitters.

— Cheers. He clinked his glass to mine and looked at me warmly across the rim of it as he drank. — You look lovely.

— What did you do today? I enquired.

— The usual. Pottered here and there. Chased up a few contacts that may shortly have land for sale. Looked at a young horse in Eillne.

— I see.

— Reggie Blood's. Good strong gelding, just broken. Popped a pole on him.

— And?

— Asked Reggie to have him dropped over.

We sat, a pitcher of cold water between us. As he ate, Ronnie mewed with pleasure.

— You know, when I told someone, can't remember who, that you cook this, they didn't believe me. They said, 'Monkfish? You must be mad!'

— Mr Wise told me about it.

— I've seen the locals throw away barrels of them on the slip. Think they're so ugly they shouldn't be eaten, Ronnie said and grinned.

— Goes to show that you should never judge by appearances.

He looked up at me sharply, then resumed his meal.

— Where's your car? I asked.

— Hmm?

— Your car.

— Oh, in Monument.

We brought down the things to the kitchen. I put the kettle on the range and husbanded a quarter spoon of precious tea into the pot.

— Why?

— Beg your pardon?

— Why did you leave your car in Monument?

— Oh, I see. Got a lift out, thought it might help the ration book.

— From whom?

— A client, or should I say, fingers crossed.

— Her car was big enough.

— Was it?

— Enormous, I would have said.

— American, so I expect it was.

We heaped the plates and dishes in a pile beside the sink. Ronnie looked at his watch. — Fancy a turn out the rock?

— Who is she?

— Oh, just someone who wants to hunt and all that. The usual. Looking for a place.

— And have you got one for her?

— Showed her a few, yes.

— Married?

— Never asked, although she's called Mrs, so I expect she must be. Now. How about it? he asked, putting his cap on.

— I don't think so, thank you.

— No?

— *No!*

Ronnie's eyes bulged. — Iz …? His mouth had dropped open. — Are you … you're not … you don't think …?

I turned away.

— Oh, God, Ronnie said. — I mean, she's just a client. She's nothing. You don't think …?

My tiredness suddenly gained the upper hand. — Of course I don't, I said and sat down.

Ronnie lurched to his knees beside me and caught my hands. — You are so beautiful, I would die, he said.

I felt my tears rise.

— Every time I see another woman, I think how lucky I am to have you, he said. — If I thought that anyone might come between us, I'd sooner jump into the sea.

CHAPTER THREE

1947–49

I loved Sibrille. We had not four seasons, but one for every day. Save for those days on which we would have been blown away like matchwood, I brought Hector out along the cliffs. It never grew cold in Sibrille. Damp, yes – water ran down the walls inside and seven months of the year, fires were lit day and night to try and keep bedding dry – but the piercing cold I had been used to, the breath-catching frosts of the midlands, were absent here. Neither did the grasses die back as they had in Meath, but accumulated on the cliffs in fat, spongy wads that Hector and I bounced on. When the tide was rising and the moon was full, whatever the time of year, we wrapped up and went out on the cliffs to watch the molten silver pour in along the causeway.

Our lives, at least Hector's and mine, seldom touched those of other people. At Christmas, we went to the Bloods

in Eillne for drinks, where I met the local curate, Father
O'Dea, a small, dark man who wore a long soutane and a
cape with an embroidered hem. It was he who encouraged
me to seek out other parts of the county, places like Leire,
a coastal spot south of Monument with cliffs even more
imposing than those of Sibrille, where one found a beach
beneath a convent and dunes that on a warm day were a
blessed place for a picnic.

The seasons seemed scarcely over till they came round
again. November sea drove mightily over the causeway.
After breakfast one Saturday, I heard activity in the yard as
Hector and I went by. Peppy was on the mounting block,
trying to sit a young horse.

— Let Roarty up first, I heard Langley say.

— Roarty's not going hunting, Peppy said.

She was fifty-five, but from the back, in her close-fitting
hacking jacket, she might well have been my age.

—Watch out! called Langley as the horse, despite Roarty
at his head, skittered away from the block, but Peppy had
sat him, side-saddle, the double reins in her quiet hands.

— Don't like his eye, Langley muttered.

♠♣

Hector was put to bed every day after his lunch, and for a
few hours, if I didn't go and lie down myself or sit reading,
I would explore the inlets and marshes around Sibrille that
were too far for the child to walk to. One afternoon in late
September, I put on boots and an old jacket of Ronnie's
and headed for the small bogs that lay on the other side of
the village, where, between September and Hallowe'en,
Peppy wildfowled with a 20-bore. From these marshy

24

places, she brought home food for two families: mallard and teal, widgeon and goose, pintail and pochard.

Ronnie was away for most of every day and often the evenings too; Langley was not someone with whom anyone could have more than a superficial relationship, I decided; and Stonely and Delaney spent much of every day playing whist in the kitchen. I had come to realise that Peppy was the core of the Shaw family and it was to her unwavering steadiness that I moored myself. She was a clever woman, far cleverer than any of the people she lived with. In Monument, she was regarded with respect, for she saw that the bills were paid mostly on time and treated everyone, no matter what their station, exactly the same. In this, I think, she had the great advantage of being English, for the English have little left to prove when it comes to Ireland, whereas the Anglo-Irish must ever strive to make the case in which they will always fail.

I had not seen Peppy shoot before, but since we had eaten our fill of her mallard on three of the five previous evenings, I thought that I would go in search of her that afternoon and get my fresh air along the string of bogs that hugged the valley. A fine, salty mist blew in off a churning sea. It was a Monday, a day on which the village was deserted since all the farmers in the area attended the Monday cattle fair in Monument. At the foot of the hill beyond the village, I crossed a stile and walked along a crooked path into the heart of the valley.

The acres to my left were hilly, to my right rushy and wet. Beyond the rushes – in reality, a river that had silted up – was poor, knobby snipe grass on which a cow and her calf stood in apparent contentment. The land gathered in a point about ten yards ahead of me. As I prepared to round it, two shots rang out, so loud they might have been inside my head. I began to shake. Two further shots exploded, deafeningly.

Of course, only moments were involved in which the first brace of wild duck had crossed Peppy's head on the far side of the point and she had dropped one. Then a further pair had risen from the reeds with the gunfire and she had killed one of those too and had then reloaded and taken the missed duck of the first pair, which had forlornly come back in search of its mate. I knew nothing of this until I felt her strong arms around me.

— I understand, my poor child, she said. — I understand.

We stayed there for a while, two women on a green, misty hillside within hearing distance of the sea. Later, we walked home, carrying the duck, and we talked. Down at the drowned soldiers' point, we sat and smoked cigarettes and talked more. Delaney took Hector for his tea and I poured gins for Peppy and me. She understood everything, and I daresay always had. I loved that woman so much. It was Peppy who saved me.

❦

Twice each season, the foxhounds met in Sibrille, the first time being in November for the opening meet. Hector and I plodded in along the causeway and up the village. Mounds of steaming dung marked the passage of horses. A trailer pulled by a tractor had come all the way from Main on the far side of Monument with the mounts of the Santrys, friends of Ronnie's whom we met occasionally. Father O'Dea had ridden over from Eillne; he sat on his cob chatting to a man called Coad, a long-established Monument solicitor whose grey mare was kept in livery by a family fallen on hard times, the Toms. The huntsman drank whiskey from little glasses brought out to him from the public house and wiped his nose on the sleeve of his scarlet jacket.

I saw Ronnie riding up the hill, smoke streaming from his jutting cigarette. He looked so distinguished. Hector and I waved, but he didn't see us. His eyes appeared to be on something in the distance and his face was set in a strange blankness.

Hounds whined and panted in a cluster at the huntsman's heels.

— Mind the child there, Ma'am, said the huntsman.

Hector, his arms about the neck of a hound, squealed as I took him out. I saw Peppy on the fringe, her veil pinned atop her silk hat, her black hunting jacket tight on her figure and her grey skirt spilling down one side of her horse's withers. The animal kept moving, never happy to stand in one place.

— Has he a kiss for Peppy? she asked as we came over.

I caught the child and hoisted him up to her, but as Peppy bent the huntsman pipped once on his horn to move off and Peppy's horse rolled its eye and reared. I snatched Hector back. As the horse dived, I saw the arc of Peppy's back, her hands up along the animal's neck. Then the steaming mass of horses, hounds and riders moved out, Peppy at the head of them, her mount back in her firm charge, dancing sideways on its four white socks. Langley came by, driven in a jeep by Roarty. I turned to point him out to Hector and realised that the child was crying.

The day turned wet. I sat reading in the lantern bay and saw Stonely, ponderous, bare headed and without a coat, walk slowly out the causeway. I thought about the blank look on Ronnie's face as he had ridden up the village hill. We had little money and this worried him, I knew. He received a tiny pension from the army for his war wound and part of the pittance that came from the letting of the fields around the lighthouse; anything else was from the commissions he received for the very occasional sale of land or from selling on a young horse that he had purchased and made into a hunter. As I sat, I heard hooves, that of a horse flat out.

My first thought was that a cliff fox, interrupted during an inland foray, was now being hunted to its earth near the sea; then I saw Peppy's horse, riderless, its single leather and iron bouncing, its double reins loose, come crashing down the steep road from the village and bolt straight out along the causeway. It was back in the yard when I reached it, creamy with sweat, feeding from a hay net. I caught its bridle and walked it to a stable, then ran out onto the causeway and listened, but could hear nothing except the tide. Hurrying back in again, I shouted to Delaney to keep an eye on Hector, then I found the keys to Ronnie's car and, praying it had enough petrol, started it up and headed for the village. If you hunted, you fell, and Peppy had hunted all her life. Sibrille was deserted. I took the Monument road, the rain slanting from the north. The horse would not have bolted for more than fifteen minutes, I imagined, trying to work out how that translated into the distance from Sibrille at which it had unseated Peppy. After another few hundred yards I saw, cantering up the grass verge towards me, Ronnie and the huntsman, their horses' ears flat. Ronnie, ashen, slid from his horse, grabbed open the car door and sat in, speechless.

He steamed. He could only point for me to drive the way he had come.

— Is she ... all right? I asked.

Ronnie's mouth hung open and his breaths came rasping. With a frantic waving of his hands, he motioned me on. I felt dread, an old feeling.

— What has happened? I cried, driving.

Ronnie shook his head, closed his eyes. A man standing by the roadside, wet hair plastered down his face, waved his arms for me to drive up a boreen. I turned, but the car's wheels skidded in muck and we slewed sideways. Ronnie was out, at the bonnet, with the man from the roadside who had run up the lane. The reverse gear roared and they pushed. The car leapt back.

— Please let me drive.

I scrambled around to get in the other door as Ronnie took my place. He reversed back out to the centre of the metal road, threw the lever into second gear and came back up the lane at speed. We careened from one limit to the other, briars scraping on both sides, the underbody grating rocks. I could see nothing for mud. Ronnie was weeping.

— Is she all right?

— The priest is with her.

— What happened?

— Fucking horse dived under a tree.

Ronnie's shoulders were heaving in distress. We began to meet horses at the head of the lane. Ronnie jumped out. I saw the riders stare at him. I pushed through and the lane opened out into a bleak, boulder-strewn field. Men stood holding clutches of horses. Fifty yards in and to one side, next to a ditch on which grew hawthorn scraws and a twisted ash, I saw a huddle, people holding an overcoat to make a canopy. Her grey skirt was spread out around her like a blanket. Langley stood to one side, his mouth spiked in the grin of his usual insouciance. It was to him I rushed, almost crying with relief, for surely Langley's unconcern meant that nothing beyond easy repair could have taken place in this damp place.

— Langley …

He turned to me, his eyes empty, his smile fixed. — What a frightful day, he said.

— Is Peppy … is she all right?

— Gone for the high jump, I'm afraid, he said.

I stared at him. I became aware of Father O'Dea beside me.

— Mrs Shaw, he said, poor Mrs Shaw is dead.

CHAPTER FOUR

1950–51

I liked the winters best in Sibrille, the really blowy months when even at low tide the sea engulfed the causeway and cut us off. At such times, the nearby village seemed like an act of folly, its houses like barnacles on the cliffs. Local people told me that after a whole winter of wind-driven sand and salt water, their eyebrows grew into crusts.

I missed Peppy. I had come to value the sight of her exercising a horse or walking down the causeway with a clump of birds in one hand, a gun in the other, or on a summer's evening on an incoming tide, standing on an utmost rock, casting for sea bass. She had fashioned her own world from Sibrille because she had had to. It was fitting, I thought, that she had died on her own terms. She would have felt nothing, the doctor said afterwards. Death had been instantaneous.

Peppy's estate was administered by her own solicitor, the

31

Mr Coad who hunted. He had been Peppy's legal advisor since she first came to Ireland and had helped her keep her finances quite separate from her husband's. Her income, which now went to Langley and Ronnie, came from canny investments made by her English north-country father. But mine was the greatest surprise: Peppy left me her house in Dublin's Ballsbridge, which was rented, by long habit, to the undersecretaries of embassies.

Peppy's money set Ronnie off on a spree. He put in central heating, something he'd seen in Dublin, and had the lighthouse painted inside and out. Without asking me, he brought in an Englishwoman who lived near Monument, a Mrs De Vere, and asked her to make loose covers for us as she had for the Santrys.

— I'd prefer it if you asked me before you arranged these things, I said.

Ronnie looked at me, surprised. — It's a business thing. I bought the De Veres their farm.

I'd come in with Hector the day before and found a small, pug-faced woman with pins in her mouth, stretched like a rubber band across our bedroom window.

— It's my house, Ronnie.

— I only wanted to surprise you.

— She's even chosen the curtain material.

— My dear, please. Ronnie could become so like Langley. — She's apparently quite famous for curtains. I mean, you've seen Main.

— I'm sure Rosa Santry did not give Mrs De Vere carte blanche, I said. — I want to be consulted.

Ronnie sighed. — As you wish.

Suddenly, we had a new Austin car, and, for the first time,

a horse trailer to go behind it. And then, one night, on the Deilt side of Monument, Ronnie almost died.

෴

He'd been driving too fast. The car had skidded off the road, then somersaulted down a ravine where, crushed and twisted, it had lain for half the night before being found. Ronnie spent six weeks in Dublin's Mater Hospital, the first two of them fighting for his life. A London neurosurgeon had flown in and operated on his head. His mouth was rebuilt. They doubted if he would ever walk again.

For days, I sat beside his hospital bed, looking at the tubes running from the head and arms, the leaping chest. During those days, both holding Ronnie's hand and in the chapel to the hospital, I prayed for his sparing so that my son could have a father and me a husband.

He went to a nursing home after the Mater and came home, a supporting plate in his mouth, ten weeks to the day of the crash. He was so thin that one could almost see through him. Three times a week, he needed to be driven into Monument for physiotherapy.

— I shall recover, you know, he said as we approached the new houses on the fringe of town. He was licking at the stiff, plastic support that held up the near side of his mouth. He said, — They say I just need time.

— Of course you will recover, I said and reached over to him. Ronnie caught my hand and kissed it, over and over.

— The thought of you and Hector kept me going, he said as we drove down Long Quay. — Even when I was out cold, I was thinking of you two.

33

— Hector is beside himself with excitement that you're home, I said.

— I've had a lot of time on the flat of my back to work things out, Ronnie said. — I need to become a lot more active in the auctioneering business.

— First of all, you need to get your full health back, I said, although since he had come home I had not shown him the pile of bills that had accumulated in his absence.

— There's big money to be made, Ronnie said. — Land is the key, mark my words.

I didn't argue, since I knew nothing about business or auctioneering; yet my own father had once been a businessman and even in ill health had demonstrated a shrewdness that Ronnie seemed to lack – which, I had to admit, was part of Ronnie's appeal.

Ronnie was not home a month when his father suffered a bad seizure. Old and very deaf, Langley had sat mostly in the sitting room of his house reading bound volumes of *Guide to the Turf*. Meals were served to him on a tray by Delaney. I could not remember the last time he and I had had a conversation. Then, one afternoon, Delaney came screaming across the narrow gap, her eyes wild. I followed her back in and passed Stonely, lurking in the hall, and saw Langley lying rigid by his armchair, his eyes fluttering and spittle in a white foam lathering his mouth.

— Oh sweet mother of God, Delaney said and fell to her knees, batting the air around his head with helpless hands. — He's dead!

He wasn't, but he would never be the same again. Medication was prescribed, but his mind, never very giving, now seemed to function less than half the time he was awake. He began to wet himself. A nurse was hired, a formidable woman who at once began to feud with Delaney. Langley's bed was moved into the sitting room, the nurse moved into Langley and Peppy's old bedroom and demanded that her meals be served in the front room, on the best china.

CHAPTER FIVE

1952–53

When Ronnie walked the farms of prospective clients or drove into Monument on provisioning trips, he had begun to take Hector with him. On dim evenings when they arrived home, glowing from the pleasure of each other, I watched in awe at the miracle that had been wrought.

Although Hector was growing up in the company of adults – instead of going to school, he was receiving lessons from a retired schoolteacher in Sibrille – I did see to it that he met other children. We were friendly with Jack and Rosa Santry, the couple who lived in Main at the other side of Monument. A few months before, when a new bridge had been built across the Thom near Main to replace the one that had been swept away in floods, it had with great ceremony been named Jack Santry Bridge. We had brought Hector to the party and he had hit it off with Kevin Santry, Jack and Rosa's son.

Ronnie had begun to advertise himself as an auctioneer in the *Monument Gazette*, the local newspaper that was read widely in the county. And, for a while, he was quite busy, selling farms by public auction, in particular those farms of deceased or otherwise departed Anglos, people he had known socially and whose relicts valued the probity of Captain Ronnie Shaw, MBVI. However, after a year of this activity, instead of simply acting as auctioneer, he went and bought the land himself, using the last of Peppy's money, with the plan to sell it on at a huge profit; alas, the client failed to spring and Ronnie was forced to unload his purchase at a loss. As if this misjudgement was not enough, however, he straight away tried to gamble his way out of the position by repeating the mistake and buying another farm. I knew nothing until he came home one day, desolate, and told me how he had been 'unlucky', the expression most used to explain a crisis. We sat on rocks watching the sea, resolute and unceasing. He had paid too much, been caught again, this time could not unload. Unlucky. The bank was demanding he sell the land for whatever he could get.

— We're in trouble, he said. — We need a breathing space.

— Might we lose the lighthouse?

—You can never tell where something like this will end.

I thought of Hector and of how happy he was growing up in Sibrille.

— There is the house in Dublin, Ronnie said.

— That was your mother's gift to me, I said gently, for I could not bear to think of selling a gift from someone so dear as Peppy.

— Of course. But perhaps it's better to have a roof over

our heads here than over someone else's head in Dublin, Ronnie said.

That night we made love in the lantern bay as seagulls with unflinching eyes hovered by the windows. Two days later, I agreed to sell the house in Dublin.

— I'll talk to Mr Coad, I said.

Ronnie made a surprised face. — We always use the other chap, what's his name. Beagle.

— Your mother used Coad.

— They're all robbers, one way or another, Ronnie said.

When I went into Monument and told old Mr Coad of my decision, he expressed the opinion that the survey map outlining the exact boundaries of the house in Dublin and its grounds was very rough and ready – good enough, perhaps, for the requirements of the time in which it had been purchased, but not up to scratch for 1953. He suggested that prior to instructing an auctioneer, a surveyor should be employed and that he would go to Dublin to instruct this person. He suggested that I come too.

❧◈❧

In order to make the eight o'clock Dublin train, we all got up at half past six and drove into Monument in the darkness. Hector was intensely wound up. He was going to stay the night at Main with Kevin Santry, his first night away from home. Ronnie, helped by Hector, carried my overnight case to the train carriage. It was early spring and people still wore their topcoats.

— Where's Coad? Ronnie asked.

— Probably on the train, I said.

Ronnie put down the case and caught me around the

waist. — You don't get up to any mischief up there, you hear? he said and made his eyes slide into the corners of their sockets.

I laughed and as we kissed I could taste salt on his lips. I suddenly hated leaving. Hector turned up his face for me and I realised that I didn't have to bend nearly as far to kiss him as I once had.

— I don't have to go … I began.

Ronnie's eyes popped. — Yes, you do! We've all got up in the dark!

We kissed again.

— I'll telephone you from my hotel before you go to bed, I promised Hector.

A tall, awkward-looking young man with large, unaligned eyes was standing at the door to the train.

— Mrs Shaw? he asked.

— I am Mrs Shaw.

— Forgive me, but I am Richard Coad, he said. — My father is unwell and has asked that I accompany you to Dublin. I am his apprentice.

I shook his hand and Ronnie bid him a gruff good morning, then the whistle sounded and I got on board and hurried to my seat so that I could wave to Ronnie and Hector through the window.

We began to move, and as Ronnie and Hector, hand in hand, tried to keep up, then fell away, Mr Coad made a fuss of putting my case up on the rack above the carriage seat and of making sure I was seated facing my preferred direction.

— Thank you, Mr Coad, I said.

He sat opposite me. — I would be extraordinarily grateful if you saw fit to call me Dick.

—Very well. On condition that you call me Iz.

He blinked and reddened. — I had no intention for a moment of suggesting ...

— It's short for Ismay, I said.

— Ah, he said, as if a long-standing question had been resolved.

Despite his age, his hairline had already begun to recede. I would not have been surprised to learn that I was the first client he had been let loose on. We chatted about Peppy's death and about the Shaws.

—The Shaws came to Ardnish in either 1673 or '74, you know, he said, lighting a cigarette. — John Shaw, an infantryman. He'd been a cooper in Devon and, it would appear, had been forced to enlist.

We were steaming through the foothills of the Deilt Mountains, past a wooded area known as Glane. Dick's uncoordinated eyes roved. His father had given him an office beside his own above the shop in Mead Street where his mother and sister sold stationery.

— Then there is a gap until 1687. John Shaw, Esquire, takes a lease of a thousand acres on the Ardnish peninsula – 'for so long as he wisheth' – from the Earl of Ardnish and Eillne – a title now long extinct – at a rent of £25 per annum, quite a lot of money in those days.

Smoke from the cigarette streamed into Dick's wild left eye as we forged through a field of white cattle.

— That's how it all began, he said, his cigarette moving with each word. — That's the Shaw history.

—You take history very seriously, Dick.

Dick clapped his chest and chuckled. — Too seriously for my own good, my mother says, always asking why I spend my time worming through parchments. I have this sense of history, ever since I first read the account of the Peloponnesian War.

The door of the carriage slid open and a steward brought in trays with tea and toast.

— The invention of history as a recorded subject, he continued and flamed another cigarette. — We're all the heirs of Thucydides, we historians, you know. The thing to remember is that at the beginning – and I'm talking about the very beginning, which is to say, let me be accurate, 431 BC – Pericles had no intention of offering battle to the Spartans. He knew he had the superior navy, so it was all down to a waiting game. Close the net at sea, block the Gulf of Corinth, Bob's your uncle. I'm boring you.

— On the contrary. Please.

— Then came the plague. Dick's young face became grim. — Is there any fairness in nature?

—Very little, I said, yet, in the end, nature is all we are left to rely on.

— I rest my case, Dick said. — One-third of all the troops died, you know, including Pericles himself. What might have happened had he lived, led on? In that aberration of nature lay the fatal undermining of the Athenian state, although it would take another twenty-seven years to come about. What statesman could have bargained for that? As he lay dying, could Pericles possibly have imagined that, in a few short years, the Persians would be funding the Spartan war effort? I mean, even Hippocrates himself could not match Pericles for vision. He was too slow, Hippocrates!

— I see.

— Thirty-five thousand Athenians killed at Syracuse alone! Dick's eyes rolled in their separate conventions. —

Are you quite sure you want to sell this property?

I stared at him. — I beg your pardon?

— It's just that, as my father explained, the house was Mrs Shaw's – that is, I should say, the late Mrs Shaw's – and thus quite separate to the collective Shaw properties, if you understand me, which may well have been why her late father, God rest him, employed my father and not Beagles to represent her, although one can never speak for the dead. And then, in her will – she was a lady for whom my father had the utmost regard – the late Mrs Shaw bequeathed the same property to your good self alone. And thus I make so bold as to wonder, if you permit, whether this decision of yours to sell is, shall I say, made in the same spirit of being separate from the collective in which it was from the outset designated and subsequently bequeathed?

Dismay rolled over me in a way for which I had not been prepared.

— Dick, I said, it has been decided.

In Dublin, we travelled by taxi from the station to Ballsbridge by way of the Shelbourne Hotel, where I was booked in. In Ballsbridge, the surveyor was waiting in his car outside the house. My house. I had never seen it before and when I got out felt a great surge of possession and, simultaneously, of loss. It was much bigger than I had imagined, one half of a solid, redbrick duo, with steep granite steps to the front door and graceful bay windows on two floors. Behind iron railings that marked the boundary of the property with the road lay a well-planted front garden. This was my house. Having scarcely seen it, I was now about to sell it.

As we made our way in along the gravel path, the surveyor, whose name was Mr Jennings, leapt ahead opening doors and then generally fretting over whether or not I might like to sit down, as if the journey thus far had exhausted me. I let him and Dick off with their maps and tapes and wandered through the house, thinking of Peppy.

The undersecretary and his family were abroad and the house was in the charge of an elderly but active woman who made me a cup of tea and spoke in warm terms about the old days. She remembered Peppy well, to my surprise, because I had not thought that Peppy had had much connection with the house beyond it being an investment.

— She used to come up to it a lot when she took it over first, the woman said. — After the war – the war here, I mean. Whenever she'd come up to Dublin, I could tell from her that there'd been trouble.

— What kind of trouble?

— Oh, the usual kind, the woman replied. — She'd say to me, 'Mrs Bailey, I hate men.' And even though with my poor husband dead I didn't have a man to love, let alone hate, I knew what she meant, God love her and be merciful to her.

The house had been Peppy's refuge from Sibrille, her own house, away from Langley and his affairs. I thought of her sitting here, where I now sat, looking out on the garden, day by day recovering her self-esteem.

— Iz?

Dick Coad's comical eyes floated around the door.

— Yes?

— Mr Jennings wondered would you do him the

honour of allowing him to bring you to afternoon tea in
the Shelbourne? Dick asked.

Mr Jennings's car crept along with great discretion.

— You can hear a watch tick, her engine is that quiet, he
told me and took out his pocket watch, which I then had
to pretend I could hear.

— She's a smashing motor altogether, Dick remarked
from the back. — Grand bit of walnut.

— A whole tree for every two cars, they say, said Mr
Jennings happily as we came to Stephen's Green.

— You got everything you need, Mr Jennings? I
enquired.

— Oh, yes. Lovely house, Mrs Shaw. Great scope to it,
the surveyor said.

— Would have stood on the edge of countryside
originally, Dick said.

— No doubt, said Mr Jennings, making way for a tram.
— They don't build them like that any more.

Swan-tailed waiters served from silver teapots into
Wedgwood in the Shelbourne's heavily draped greenroom.
Pages wandered in and out singing messages in falsetto as
Mr Jennings told us about his eldest daughter, married to
a senior policeman in Nottingham, and how he, Mr
Jennings, with Mrs Jennings, had been introduced to the
Lord Mayor and how they had travelled, courtesy of the
Lord Mayor, in his Bentley all the way to the boat in
Liverpool.

— Nottingham, said Dick, warming up. — What did you
think of the cathedral?

— We didn't get Mass in Nottingham, said Mr Jennings.
— Some more tea, Mrs Shaw?

I sat forward. — Isn't that my name?

I beckoned the page.

— Mrs Shaw?

— I'm Mrs Shaw.

— Telephone call, madam.

I followed him out and down a corridor to a line of little wooden cabins with glass doors. Behind a counter, women in headsets worked tangled, eel-like lines of telephone cables.

— Hello? I said, closing the door to one cabin.

— Iz?

— Who is it?

— This is Rosa. Hector told me where you were staying, but …

— Hello?

— I don't want you to be alarmed because I'm sure there's nothing too badly wrong, but Hector's got a knock on his head.

I saw, through the glass, the women's speeding hands, arranging, rearranging.

— Oh, God. Is he …?

— Jack's brought him to the hospital. They're keeping him overnight, simply a precaution, I'm sure. We've tried to send word to Ronnie.

There was no telephone in Sibrille.

— He's probably out showing land, I said. — Oh my God. Is he conscious?

— He … Her voice faded, resurged. — … his eyes.

— I'm sorry, I can't hear! Is Hector conscious?

The phone seemed dead. I shook it, crazily.

— Iz? Are you there?

— His eyes? What about his eyes?

— ... fell off Kevin's pony. You mustn't be alarmed. My husband — one of you ...

All I could think of was fishermen and eels. — But is he conscious?

— He was ...

She went into the far distance again. I kicked open the door.

— She's gone! I cried and the telephone women turned and stared at me.

— ... the doctor said. Iz?

I was suffocating so much that I could hardly hold the telephone. I said, — I'm coming home.

The last train to Monument had left. Although I wanted to hire a taxi, Mr Jennings would hear none of it. I was too shocked to argue. Dick Coad saw us off, the unfixed pupils of his eyes at large. He had papers to file the next morning in the Four Courts, he said, otherwise he too, in the circumstances, would have returned to Monument. He had spent a fruitless fifteen minutes trying to get through to the hospital.

— I shall say a decade of the rosary, he said and I saw my own face reflected in the car's window, hand to my throat.

— She'll have us there in under four hours, Mr Jennings said as we met the flat, open countryside. — She's made for a trip like this.

From the moment he had been born, it had been my greatest dread. Now it was as if I had long foreseen this day, as if my terror, and the fact that I could move my limbs only with difficulty and the clutch in my breast had all been reheased.

We stopped for refreshments in a midlands town. Mr Jennings had spoken almost non-stop since our departure, not in an intrusive way, but in a low drone as if a wireless were turned on in another room. His wife was from Belfast, her father had been a minister, there was murder when she married Mr Jennings, a Catholic. They went to India in 1929. He asked the girl behind the till for a receipt for the pot of tea and we resumed our journey.

—You take life as it comes, he said, a repeated theme. — You treat it decent and life obliges you, as a rule.

It was still light as we came in by Deilt. I craved Ronnie. He would be at the hospital, by Hector's bed, and I would have someone into whose arms I could fall. The hospital, built on the Deilt road, was almost the first building in Monument one came to from the Dublin direction. We swept in around a circular flowerbed to the front doors and, as I got out, I smelled new-mown grass, the first cut of that year. The porter saw me and came out from his desk. My legs were going.

— Mrs Shaw.

I had no idea how he knew me, discovered days later that he was from Sibrille.

— Is my husband here?

— No, Ma'am, but the little fellow is fine, he said.

— Oh, thank God!

He was supporting my elbow as we proceeded down a corridor of blinding lights.

— Gave us all a fright. Mrs Santry herself came in with him, there was a sight of blood, but it just goes to show, the more blood the better is often the way, the porter said.

I could not work it out. — Has my husband been in?

47

— No, Ma'am, although we sent a message to the post office in Sibrille, the porter said. — We didn't want to send a telegram – think of the fright the poor man would get. Now, here we are.

I went into the room and saw Hector in an enormous bed, his head bandaged, his thumb in his mouth, asleep.

— Hector.

I held him for my life. He opened his eyes and smiled.

— He can see me! I cried.

— There, now. A nurse wearing a silver badge was beside me. — He's a little rascal, there's no doubt. Aren't you a rascal, Master Shaw?

— I was riding Kevin's pony, Hector whispered and went back to sleep.

— He's bound to be exhausted, and so are you, Mrs Shaw, the nurse said. — We heard from Mrs Santry that you were in Dublin.

— Oh my God! I cried. — I never thanked Mr Jennings.

No breath of wind disturbed the surface of the sea. It seemed bizarre that in the sixteen hours since I had left, so much had taken place, yet Ronnie was still unaware. I was glad for him. When I told him, he would, despite how late it was, want to drive into Monument to see Hector, but none of the agony of my journey would attend his.

The headlamps of the hackney swept the still water as we came down the causeway. No life was evident in the windows of either the lighthouse or Langley's. I felt emptied to a place of peace and exhaustion, as if I had walked twenty miles. So grateful, too, for all the many kindnesses I had been shown. To have been anxious about a house — a mere house, whatever its provenance — seemed profane in the face of what had nearly been. I promised myself to never again be concerned about possessions. We had something rare and wonderful, Ronnie, Hector and I.

The driver pulled up beside Ronnie's car and brought my suitcase up the steps to the door. I stood and watched as he drove up into the village and then back into the mass of the land, his lights fading. Voices drifted down to me, people leaving the pub in Sibrille, their cheery 'goodnights' or the growl of a tractor, the transport for many. I often stood out here like this, alone, on the edge, the voices and sounds of the village a tenuous connection, yet a connection all the same to something essential that we were not quite part of.

I brought in my suitcase, closed the door. Coals glowed in the range. I heard movement upstairs. Ronnie must have been tired and had gone to bed early. I put the light on and filled the kettle to make tea for us, for I knew he would get a shock when he heard the news.

— Ronnie! A voice in the kitchen could be heard clearly overhead. — It's me, darling!

Then I saw a page of notepaper lying on the table beside its torn envelope. I saw the stamp of Sibrille's post office and that day's date.

Dear Captain Shaw,
Your son has been in a riding accident. Please contact the hospital in Monument.
Sincerely,
G. Mather (Postmaster)

I stood there, trying to work it out: how could Ronnie

49

have read this note and not gone into Monument? His car was parked outside. How could he be in bed knowing Hector was in hospital? And then, as if volts were passing through my head, I heard another voice in our bedroom.

Shouting, I ran upstairs. As I came to our bedroom door, a low-sized, ghost-like figure clutching up a bed sheet went to pass me. I screamed. I tore the sheet away and stared at the defiant, pug-like face. I screamed and screamed as Ronnie pushed by me with armfuls of their clothes and went down the stairs. The smell of her in my bedroom. I could hear them going out the door. I flung open the windows and dragged over the bedding and, screaming, pitched everything into the sea. I could hear the car leaving. It was not just that I had caught him, but that he had elected to fornicate here rather than drive into Monument and be with Hector. Enraged, I hurled Ronnie's shirts, shoes, ties, hunting clothes and boots into the Atlantic. I screamed. I threw out his brushes and silver dressing-table accoutrements, his entire drawers of socks and handkerchiefs and underwear. I threw every trace of him into the sea. Were it not for the splinter of reason that told me that my son needed me, I would have thrown myself.

CHAPTER SIX

1953–54

The sea ran all the way to the moon in endless corrugations. I slept, then sometime in the small hours, putting on a jacket and shoes, I went downstairs and out. Without a moon, the cliff would have been dangerous, but, on such nights, every hillock and blade of dew-shimmering grass was picked out with remorseless clarity. At the very apex of the rise, at the point where if one went any farther, sight of the lighthouse was lost, I put down. Over my left shoulder, if I turned, the light in the lantern bay glowed as if a secret were trapped in the deep.

Ronnie had moved out of the lighthouse and into the boxroom in Langley's. I refused to speak to him, so instead, he wrote to me, long, rambling letters full of remorse. Although he did not go so far as to blame the other woman for what had happened, knowing I would think even less of him for attempting that, he did nonetheless insist that the evening had been impromptu.

I sat on the cliff and wondered about life's apportion-
ment. I would never really forgive Ronnie, I knew; but,
then, life is a constant compromise with disappointment
and imperfection.

The change from night to dawn came when the moon
was still quite high and was attended by a breeze from the
east. Seabirds grumbled in the cliff below my feet and
began to scatter outwards. Nothing dramatic occurred,
no red ball of fire or the like; rather, more a gradual
yellowing along the length of the eastern horizon and an
ebbing of the black making way to blue, the sudden surge
of the tide's voice at dawn and the screech of oyster
catchers.

Ronnie's innate pomposity could not be concealed,
even by his contrition: were I to give him another chance,
I would discover how incredibly committed he was to
our marriage and our love, he wrote. His letters travelled
all the way from Sibrille into Monument and out again to
the lighthouse.

I watched as black divers took shape and worked the
surface of the sea. The wind stayed in the east, bringing
with it an edge of coldness. I raised my face to catch the
sun's weak but precious heat. As the wind stiffened,
whitecaps in their thousands appeared below me.

☙❧

After three months, it was because of Hector that I finally
allowed him back. He brought a camp bed with him and
slept in the downstairs room. We had to discuss such
things as where Hector was going to go to school and

about the fact that I had decided not to sell my house in Dublin. As the months went by, we fell back into our routines.

He had become employed by a firm of Monument auctioneers, Gargan & Co., which was owned by a man whom I had formerly heard Ronnie describe as a corner boy. Now, Ronnie conducted auctions on his behalf. I could understand why Mr Gargan would want to employ someone like Ronnie: the Anglo-Irish voice and the clear, unflinching stare over a room full of prospective buyers embodied integrity as far as the native Irish, long confused in these matters, would see it. Ronnie drew a salary – the first Shaw ever to do so – and Gargan & Co. provided him with a motor car.

❧

Ronnie's neurosurgeon came to fish in May. Mr Hedley Raven had drilled holes in Ronnie's head with the result that Ronnie could walk – a miracle, according to Dr Armstrong, our local GP, who had read Hedley Raven's account of Ronnie's case in the *British Medical Journal*. I helped Delaney clean out a room in the coastguard house and put a bed into it and opened the windows and hung curtains. The Englishman arrived by taxi from Monument with three sets of rods in canvas holders and associated leather boxes and canvas bags.

— My wife, Iz, Ronnie said.

The doctor removed his cap. When I saw his fair hair, I realised for the first time that Ronnie was now almost grey.

— Iz?

— It's short for Ismay.

— I like Iz, he said.

— I hope you catch lots of fish, I said.

He and Ronnie went to the rocks, where they stayed until midnight, fishing the incoming tide. The next morning, I cooked one of their sea bass for breakfast.

— You don't fish? the doctor asked.

— No. My mother-in-law tried to teach me, but I was hopeless, I said.

— It's all a matter of concentration, he said. His eyes were at the limit of blue where it becomes black. — You have to think like a fish. You have to surrender yourself to your instincts. Once you've learned to do it, then it's simple.

— Where do you fish in England? Ronnie asked.

— More in Scotland, on the Tay, Hedley Raven said. — But this sea stuff is like starting all over again.

— I spent some of the war near the Tay, Ronnie said.

— How do you find the time? I asked. — Between operating and writing articles?

— Aha, someone's been talking! the doctor said.

— Our local GP.

— A dreadful busybody, Ronnie said. — You couldn't keep the man in whiskey.

— He obviously reads, Hedley said. — I like that in a GP.

— I've some business near Deilt this morning, Ronnie said. — Do you mind if I leave you to the mercy of my wife?

The days were hurtling out into endless unfoldings of light. When Hector had gone to his tutor in the village, I walked along the cliff top. Far out on a tiny rock, I could see Hedley, the sea churning white up around his thigh waders. He cast easily, his body flexing back and forth. His wife too was a doctor, he had said, working long hours in a hospital in London. They had no children, by fate or design he gave no indication. I tried not to dwell on who he reminded me of, for I knew that texture of fair hair, I knew the full feel of it in my fists. I took up my book and tried to read. Of course, Hector had such fair hair, and so too had I.

— Hector's like you, Hedley remarked later, putting down a framed photograph.

— D'you think so? Ronnie thinks he's the image of him.

— I've always wanted a son, he said.

I turned and found him looking at me calmly.

— My wife doesn't want children, he said.

— I see.

— I dream of having a son and of passing on everything I know to him.

— And what would that be? I asked, resuming my carrot chopping. — Medicine?

— Oh, more important things than medicine. How to fish on a dry fly. How to respect other people. How to appreciate women.

I didn't have to look again to see the colour of his eyes. I asked,

— Is that really possible? I mean, to teach a child, do you think?

— You mean about women?

— Ah, yes, I said and felt myself go on fire.

He laughed. — Of course. The world is full of beauty and women are the proof of it.

— And would you teach him to say that to every

woman he met? I asked, trundling all the carrots into the stock pot.

— Only to those in lighthouses, Hedley replied.

❧

Bibs Toms came to supper to make up our numbers. Her mother had died and Bibs had reared her infant sister and worked shoulder to shoulder with their father, keeping horses in livery. At thirty-two, having decided that the way forward was to shock, Bibs had become the gal who leapt tables at hunt balls, drank gin and spoke her mind even when it was quite empty.

— I'm terrified of doctors. I mean, how can you trust them? she asked.

— If I hadn't trusted this one, I'd be in a wheelchair, Ronnie said. A plastic support was still needed to keep up one side of his mouth.

— Our local witch doctor has hands as cold as cucumbers, Bibs said and shivered.

— I hear he's a good man, said Hedley. — Reads up his stuff.

— He's what the locals call a 'dthreadful man' for his whiskey, said Bibs, performing. — Daddy was ill a few years ago and Dr Armstrong arrived around midnight to see him, so tight he could hardly walk, let alone drive, winking like bejasus at me. Left me two pills for Daddy, a small, fat one and a long, oblong one. 'Get him to take one of each, sweetheart,' he said.

Bibs leaned back, guffawing. — 'Get him to take one of each, sweetheart!'

I ladled out second portions of stew.

—What are the odds of Ronnie getting back on a horse for the opening meet? enquired Bibs.

Hedley was stern. — Not for a year at least, he said.

— Spoilsport! Bibs cried.

Ronnie shot a crooked grin at her. — Maybe you can bring me for a gentle hack coming up to Christmas.

Bibs rolled her eyes. — *Pas de problème,* she said theatrically.

Hedley topped up his glass from the large, amber ale bottle.

—You don't hunt either, Iz? he asked.

— No, I don't hunt. Either. Nor do I shoot.

— I'm sorry, I didn't mean to …

— I love this place in my own way, thank you, I said and knew I sounded angry.

Ronnie looked at me and his eyes were cold.

— I hear you're going fishing in Main tomorrow, Bibs beamed into the sudden pool of silence. — Lucky you. Last of the great Irish houses and all that tosh. In fact, the Santrys aren't at all bad.

— I can't wait, Hedley said.

— Rosa's a stunner, said Bibs, as would a man.

— She's a lovely person, I said.

— Early start then, said Hedley. — Hard work, all this enjoying yourself, eh?

— We'll leave before eight, Ronnie said. He looked to Bibs. — Don't feel like carrying the doctor's rod tomorrow, do you?

— I don't think I'd be up to it, gasped Bibs in mock exhaustion and Ronnie turned so red with laughter I thought he'd got a piece of stew stuck in his windpipe.

But the next morning after breakfast, just before they set

out, Mr Gargan the auctioneer turned up and told Ronnie that a group of Germans had arrived and wanted to look at land.

— I'll run you over to Main, but I'll not be able to stay and fish, Ronnie said.

— That's ridiculous, I said. — You go with Mr Gargan, I'll drive Hedley to Main.

— I don't have to fish in Main, said Hedley.

— Of course you do, I said.

— Here's hoping I land a few myself, said Ronnie, hurrying out.

❧

We entered Main by way of its massive, eagle-topped entrance gates. The long avenue, over a mile, led eventually to the enormous house, where the doors were always open but one rarely found anyone in. Dogs and peacocks sprawled in the sunshine and showed no interest in our arrival. From the shadows stepped a yard man in a cloth cap who told us that he had been instructed to walk us down to the river. He picked up Hedley's baskets and bags and we set out.

— You sure you want to do this? Hedley asked. — It's very boring if you don't fish.

— I've brought a book, I said.

We walked down through a tall meadow and into a wood. The coolness was immediate. Pigeons thrashed out of high foliage and a fox slunk from a pile of ferns and trotted away before us, its tail brushing the ground. The path wound ever down, tree roots breaking upwards like ribs. I could hear the water before I saw it, its race over stones, and the deep sound of insects, absent beside the sea. The farm hand walked backwards so that branches were held for us and I stepped out into the heat of the river's bank.

Few stretches of salmon water in Ireland could compare with the one beside which I lay in the shade, reading. The man who had brought us down had spent some time showing Hedley the spots at which to cast, then he had left. Upstream from where I had put down, the river curled out of sight and deepened. I saw Hedley's cloth-capped head bob its way out of my line of vision, the curls at his neck becoming indistinct. I liked watching him, as I had the day before from the cliff. I liked to savour the bending of his upper body, the angle of his head, the deftness of his hands. He was gentle and caring, I was sure. I thought of the previous evening and of the coldness in my husband's eyes. I could suddenly and vividly imagine Hedley's body, it's curves and lengths, its strength.

— A penny for your thoughts.

— How did you …?

— The river doubles back around the wood, he said, sitting beside me. — Besides, any fish worth catching is asleep in this heat.

I was sure that he had been observing me for some time and now it felt as if he must have been able to read my thoughts. I said — Would you like some tea?

I took out cups and unscrewed the flask. As he held out his cup, I could see the race of blond hairs across the bone of his wrist.

— Isn't it just lovely here? I said, as I tried to gather myself.

— It could not be lovelier, he said, looking at me. He sat, his hands about his knees. — May I say something?

— By all means.

—You are so beautiful it makes me want to weep.

I sat back. — I'm sorry, but what an extraordinary thing to say.

— I want to weep because it's a crime to leave you so unhappy.

I stared at him, wondering if the heat had made me dizzy.

— Unhappy?

—Yes. He took my hand and kissed it. —Very.

I drew back to find my breath. — That's enough, I think.

— I don't.

We were kissing. First we kissed as we knelt, then he pressed me gently back and we kissed as we lay on the rug. I could not hold him tight enough, nor taste deeply enough of his mouth. The smell of the sweat from his flannel shirt. The feel of his face to my hands, its warm coarseness, his weight, his recklessness. His hands were on my bare legs.

— No!

I sat up.

— Iz …

— This is insanity! Anyone could walk out and find us. Ronnie is due here any moment.

— Iz, I want you to come back to England with me.

I stared. — I've hardly met you.

He took my hands in his. — Love takes no account of conventions. Do you love Ronnie?

I was distracted and shook my head. — I'm married to Ronnie.

—Why did you marry him?

I couldn't breathe. — Because I … I wanted to.

— There! You didn't say, 'I married him because I love him.'

I took away my hands.

He said, — And I'm married to a woman who's agreed to divorce me. Look, Iz, although I've hardly met you, perhaps that is why I can see things as they are. You're trapped in a marriage without love. I saw his eyes last night. Tell me I'm wrong!

— We're just going through a difficult period. He nearly died not so long ago, as you well know.

— He doesn't appreciate or deserve you. Tell me you're happy with him and I won't say another word.

I found myself being swept away by a force that I knew I could not resist.

— I'm forty-two, Hedley said urgently. — I've got everything in life except love. I think I've found it here. Look at me, Iz. He caught my hand up and brought it to his cheek. — I'll look after everything, employ the best solicitors. I'll take six months off and we'll sail around the world. Then, when we come back, we'll live wherever you please.

Despite myself, I began to believe that what he was proposing was actually possible. I asked,

— What about Hector?

— He comes with us, of course.

— He loves his father.

— It's not difficult any more to get from here to England. He can divide his time during the holidays. He can do whatever he wishes.

He wiped my eyes. I turned away. — I can't.

— Iz, Iz. I know nothing about your life, but I'm prepared to bet it hasn't been easy, that you've had more than your share of disappointments. I want to dedicate myself to making that up to you, to making you happy, whatever it takes, because all it takes is love. This is not outrageous. It is not wrong to want to be happy. People do it the whole time.

— You're mad, I said and blew my nose. — I think I am too.

— Was that madness when we kissed? he asked. — Or was that the sanest moment of our lives?

I looked up. — Oh, God, here's Rosa Santry.

She was walking from the far end of the bank, her son at her side.

— Iz. He gripped my arm. — Think about everything I've said. Please. I've never in my life been more sober or serious. I love you. I want you forever. I realise that you can't drop everything tomorrow and jump on the train with me, but think about it. Please.

Rosa was no more than fifty yards away.

I said, — Yes.

❧

I spent the next three weeks in turmoil. Often I saw myself in the bedroom mirror and wondered if I looked hard enough if I might see the demon that had entered me. For no matter how hard I tried, even to the extent of relieving my own want, I couldn't erase my passion. I had heard it said that, in order for love to be lastingly successful, you have to again and again find a new person within yourself, but I could not reach anywhere within me without touching Hedley. He became fused in my mind with desire lost and squandered happiness. I had not even trusted myself to say goodbye to him, but had gone out and sat on the cliff, something Ronnie had found ill mannered and had been short with me about. But the previous night, Hedley had slipped me a note with the date when he was coming to Dublin for a medical conference and had begged me to meet him there.

I was swamped alternately by guilt and desire. I saw my lovely son and told myself how he would be even happier if his mother was the new Mrs Hedley Raven. I saw Ronnie, limping, and the pain it was for him still to drive a car and go about his poky business, and I was swept by the meanness of what I intended. It was neither my fault nor Ronnie's that the right chemistry had not fermented between us. I kept seeing the coldness in his look, something I would never have imagined possible. Although he would be distraught for a time when I left him, I at least would be happy, surely a better position for both of us than mutual indifference. But was I indifferent, or just drenched by lust? I decided firmly not to go to Dublin, changed my mind twenty times, laughed at my ability to destroy everything I so much cherished, made a dental appointment in Monument for the day in question so that I would not be able to travel; then, with three days to go, said to Ronnie, — I think I'd like to go to Dublin to check the house.

He looked at me, but if he knew it was my first outright lie to him, then it was not apparent.

— Good idea, he said. — Bring Hector.

— He gets too tired, I said. — Next time, when he's a bit older.

— Stay the night, Ronnie said. — Up and down in one day takes too much out of you.

❧

I boarded the train at eight o'clock and as we reached the foothills and gathered speed, I saw my face reflected in the carriage window and thought of another journey in the opposite direction when I had set out with similar guilt at what I was leaving behind. And as before, as if I were too insubstantial to have abiding concerns, my guilt shrank with each mile and my point of longing grew. In the taxi on the way to the hotel on the Liffey beside the Four Courts, I slipped off my wedding band. Hedley was waiting. He looked anxious, as if he had not really believed that I would come.

— I have a room, he said.

I went deaf as we went up the stairs together, not just because of a sense of perfect re-enactment, but because I was terrified. On the landing, Hedley took my hand in his. I clung to him. The room was large with two long windows. A wide, brass double bed stood in the centre, as if on a stage. There was a strange bareness that took me some seconds to come to terms with.

— Where are your things? I asked, for his medical conference was to run over three days.

— I thought you might prefer it if I did not stay here, he whispered. — That it might look better.

I had dreamed of this, of being alone with him in such a room. I sank into his arms and smelled him again, and then, as if haste were all, we were shedding clothes, mouths together, and I felt his flesh against me, his great need, which matched mine, but time was not there for such reflection since I lay back beneath him on the bed and felt myself move at such speed from his mere touch that I spilled over, as did he, his fingers over my mouth, and the backs of my eyes exploded.

Hedley poured tea, his hand steady. He carried over the cup and saucer to the bed. I could have lain there and watched him forever.

— You're spoiling me, I said.

He was beautiful, limb perfect and his skin gleamed. He bent down and kissed me.

— What about your conference? I asked.

— Doesn't start till six.

— Where is it?

— In the Gresham.

Getting into bed, he worked himself behind me so that I sat in his lap. In the branches of a tree outside our window, a blackbird hopped.

— I have lots of questions, I said.

— You're not to worry.

— I'm not. I've never been happier.

— You and I are one now. It's good.

I ached anew for him, but the rational part of me demanded that the disorder I was leaving in Sibrille be at least partially tidied.

— I want to talk about Hector.

— We'll discuss Hector this evening. This time is for you and me.

He began to kiss my neck, to run his tongue into the little furrow at the base of my hairline. I bent forward and he kissed the knobs at my spine's top, licking each round and making a slow descent until I had to arch my back to release the sudden, unexpected gush of pleasure. His deft hands moved to my belly and then, down, and he brought me up a notch with his quick but subtle fingers.

— Kneel!

I did and reached back for him and he was there in full again, thick to my hand. He cupped my thighs and pulled them wide. I knew suddenly what he was going to do, but craved it as if nothing was too debased or unworthy. He splayed me further and I ached in my deepest pith to have him where no one had ever been, for this was the most I could give. I heard him spit into his hand, then he came up and began to enter, and pleasure and pain then were almost too much as he strained and I had to grip the bed end with both hands and his mouth was in my hair as he shouted out, — *Oh, God!*

We must have slept, for I awoke with a start and saw him dressed at the bed end, staring at me.

—You are beautiful, he said.

—Where are you …?

— Sleep. Your doctor prescribes it.

I reached out. I was sore, but it was a happy soreness, as if between us we had initiated something and my mark of it was my proof of love. He caught my wrist, kissed it.

—What time … ?

— Shh! I'll order a late supper to be brought up.

He left noiselessly and I went back to sleep. It was a sleep without dreams, a profound immersion in all the forces that had brought me to this point, as if I were being transported across dark waters, sailing between points only visible to sea things. Darkness was absolute. I awoke to it.

— Hedley?

He was in the bed beside me, had come in when I was asleep and had not wanted to waken me; of this I was sure, because I could smell him. I put on the light. The vastness of the room and my solitary presence made my throat catch. I looked around, since maybe he was somewhere else in there, or hiding. Then I saw the time. Four in the morning. I got up and washed. I was much sorer, but now the prize seemed suddenly inexplicable. I thought of Hector and began to shake. Splashing water on my face, I tried to rinse Hector away and concentrate. Dressed, I went downstairs. The night porter, woken from sleep, leapt to his feet.

— Ma'am?

— Has there been anyone here looking for me? Mrs Shaw.

The man scratched his head and rubbed his sleepy eyes.

— Divil a one since I came on, Ma'am.

I tried to think. — I want to go to the Gresham Hotel. Please call me a taxi.

— God, Ma'am, it's four in the morning.

— Call me a taxi!

It was after five when the taxi left me off in O'Connell Street. The Gresham ran to two night porters, both of them in livery and more alert than the one I'd left. They needed to unbolt the hotel's door.

— I have an important message for a Mr Raven, I said. — Mr Hedley Raven. He's staying here.

They brought me in and one of them went behind a desk. — Mr ...?

— Raven, I said, Hedley Raven. He's a doctor, he's here for the medical conference.

— That conference finished yesterday at lunchtime, the porter said. He turned the page of his book. — Dr and Mrs Raven, here they are. Checked out at six yesterday evening. They went to the mail boat. Miss?

The other one had caught me. It wasn't my head, it was just my legs that would not work.

— It's all right, Miss.

I saw his concerned face.

— It's Mrs, I said.

CHAPTER SEVEN

1958

Whenever I dwelled on what I had done in Dublin, it swept me with shame. Not alone the shame of having been so used and the manner in which that had occurred, or the shame of my own gullibility, but shame on a deeper level. I had taken the awe-inspiring love I had once known and debased it. That I could have soiled something so precious and been so blind to its need for nurturing drove me to the very edge of reason. I had shamed myself and, in the process, had shamed the dead.

As time went by, however, it slowly became clear that what I had done might well have saved my marriage. For Ronnie knew nothing of Dublin or the Four Courts Hotel and thought that my humours all sprang from womanly moods. My own behaviour had forced me to reconsider my opinion of him and to accept that if he had succumbed to a moment of indiscretion, then I, by my deliberate intent,

69

had exceeded his impropriety by a distance. It was of no use to try and defend my actions by saying that Ronnie had driven me to them, or to plead justification for myself while condemning him. We were both human beings who had erred and who now had to make the best of what we had. Our relationship would be decent and dignified and would stand alone without reference or comparison to other experience. I would apply myself anew, forgetting every-thing that had gone before.

⧡

At thirteen, Hector was as tall as me and up to Ronnie's shoulder. He now attended a tiny school in Monument, set up and paid for by the Catholic merchants of the town, but, soon, he would have to go away to secondary school, something I had been preparing for. Ronnie and I would then be alone in the lighthouse.

One evening in mid-August, when Delaney and I were spending most of every day sewing name tags onto his clothes, Hector came in to where his father and I were sitting and said, — I don't want to go to school in England.

— Oh, it'll be fine, don't you worry, Ronnie said. — I remember feeling exactly the same before I left Gortbeg.

His mouth no longer needed the plastic support, but his face had set into a permanently skewed, almost fractured, look that, sometimes, in brief, unexpected moments, made him seem like a complete stranger.

Hector said, — I don't mind leaving home, it's just I don't want to go to England.

— Well, I'm afraid, sir, that's a pity, but you don't have

any more choice in the matter than I did. Sorry, old boy.

— I'm not going.

— I don't wish to discuss it, Hector.

— Hector, why? I asked.

— Only the real West Brits are still doing it, none of my friends are. They're all going to school in Dublin.

— And learning gobbledygook, Ronnie said.

— The people who still go come back to Ireland and have no friends here, Hector said. — A friend of mine in school has a sister who got married last year and she'd been to school in England. There wasn't a single guest at the wedding who lived in Ireland.

— Thinking of getting married, are you, old boy? Think carefully, if I was you, Ronnie drawled.

He had the Anglo-Irish tendency not to engage the specific, to reduce an issue to its most trivial and to forestall the inevitable by refusing to recognise it.

— I'm not going.

— You've always been happy up to now about going, Hector. Everything's arranged. Isn't it a bit late to say this? I asked.

— Excuse me, but I don't see the point of a discussion which may give rise to false hope, said Ronnie. — Leave it, shall we?

— I'm discussing something with Hector.

— Which I deem most unwise.

— Nonetheless, I'm still discussing it.

— I forbid it.

— You ... what?

— You heard me.

I closed my eyes for a moment. — Hector, please leave the room.

— If you're discussing me, I want to be here, said Hector.

— Please.

— I'm not going.

— *Leave the room!*

I was trembling as the boy left, shaking his head.

Ronnie looked at me with a supercilious expression. — Congratulations.

— How dare you! Is that all you can offer him when something huge in his life arises? A patronising smirk? 'Thinking of getting married, are you, old boy?' What kind of a father are you?

— He's a child, Ronnie sighed, weary of the matter.

— He's highly intelligent. What's wrong with what he said? What's wrong with going to school in Ireland? There must be half a dozen suitable schools. Why does he absolutely have to go to England just because you did?

— And my father, and his father.

— So?

Ronnie's eyes emptied. — Tradition may well have ended in your family with you, but here we still value it.

— What a despicable thing to say! You're not capable of discussing the matter on its own merits without dragging in a personal attack!

— Does what I say not reflect the truth? Did you not ensure that everything your family held dear would end in one most unlovely debacle?

— You ... pig!

— Am I?

— I hate you, Ronnie.

— Is that all you can say?

— What on earth does my family matter when it comes to deciding where Hector should go to school? For that matter, why should the fact that you and his grandfather went to one school mean that Hector must now go there too? I think, in fact, he's right. This is Ireland, our own country. Why must everything still relate to England? You're out of touch.

— We're talking not just about tradition, but about standards, about the type of person you want as your friend, about connections. You think he'll get that in any school here?

— The point he makes is that he will. What connections did you make that are now so vitally important?

— More than you imagine, Ronnie said, getting up and looking at his watch. — Now, if you'll excuse me, I have business to attend to.

— You're ridiculous. We live here in a tiny lighthouse, we own less than half of the land we did when I married you, we must watch how every penny is spent, you dart here and there like a mouse, trying to be the first to latch on to the newest person who comes into the area and has money. A lot of good going to school in England did you!

Ronnie turned, his misaligned face all at once white and set.

— If you'd had any style, we mightn't be as we are. You let us all down, every day, simply by being you.

— What did you say?

— You heard me.

I caught up a cup and hurled it; it bounced from his shoulder and smashed on the floor.

— Get out!

Ronnie stopped, then, eyes wild, he went to the stove, snatched up the pot of soup and hurled it out through the open window into the sea. I picked up a vase and launched it for his head; although he ducked, it caught him high on his temple before disintegrating against the wall. Ronnie, panting, began to throw the furniture the same way as he had the soup. Picking up a heavy chair, I flung it at him, my strength a wonder. The chair caught him full square and he went down, winded. I picked up the breadboard, a generous piece of polished walnut, and went to stave in his head, but he caught my ankles and dragged hard so that I fell back and the board merely hit him in the chest. As if he had been interrupted in some serious task, Ronnie scrambled up and began to pitch every item of cutlery, glassware and crockery out the other kitchen window, many of them landing on his car that was parked below. I was bleeding from my mouth, yet I felt strangely empowered and elated. I picked up a pot stand and made a run at him. Ronnie went down again. I kicked him hard in the jaw. He winced and I wondered if I'd undone all the work of the unspeakable Mr Hedley Raven. I drew back again to kick harder.

— *Stop!*

I froze. Hector was standing there.

— You've both gone mad!

The boy's eyes were huge. Each time I tried to take a breath, my chest screamed.

— It's all right, Hector, said Ronnie, getting up, wincing. — We were just airing our differences.

Hector looked from one of us to the other.

— And have you stopped now?

— Have we stopped now? Ronnie asked, his teeth bared in pain.

—Yes, we have stopped now, I panted.

❧

In the months that followed, when Hector had gone away to school in England and I was forced to confront my true feelings for my husband, I always came back to our fight that day and, when I did, I always smiled. Like a storm that clears the atmosphere, I had felt immeasurably the better of it. My head was clear and, for the first time in years, I was happy. Although the gaps between our lovemaking were irregular – in itself not unusual for a marriage of a dozen years, I had read – Ronnie's stamina on those occasions was always short, something I could live with, but with which, I imagined, a succession of mistresses might be impatient. I tried to remember him as I had first met him, his nonchalance with the everyday things of life, his sense of humour and his easy charm. For despite everything, we still had times of sweetness together. They coincided in the main with Ronnie's business catastrophes. Stripped of his tricks by worry and impending disaster, I saw another Ronnie, devoid of winning ways or the need to dissemble. My wish in those times was perverse: that we could always be like this, an aspiration which involved never-ending misfortune; but at least then I would have him alone, which is to say, a man without pretensions, in need of love, who stayed at home and close to me, who came out the cliffs for walks and who listened as well as spoke.

❧

— Hector's getting on well.

We inched through a herd of port-bound cattle at the top of Captain Penny's Road.

— He likes his school.

— Not right for an only child to be at home on his own. Needs company.

— His every move is a mirror of you.

— Boys are like that. I remember how it was with my own father. Wanted to be him.

We made our way forward as drovers beat and shouted.

— May I say something? Ronnie asked. — I'd like to start again, you and me. From scratch. Go back to the very beginning. What do you say?

I could not conceal my frustration. — I don't know, Ronnie. Really, I don't.

— Please.

— I'll think about it, I said.

A few nights later, I was reading in bed when a knock came to the door of the lantern bay.

— May I come in?

It was clear Ronnie had been drinking – not a common occurrence, but now manifested in a fixed, Langley-type grin. He sat on the side of my bed.

— Big changes.

— Oh?

— You know. Me drawing a wage, Langley peeing himself, Hector gone. Big, big changes.

— Change can be good.

Ronnie grinned. — You don't change, though. You just get more beautiful.

I felt my eyes brim. Ronnie sat on the bedside, then bent down and we kissed.

— That was good, he said.

— Yes.

— D'you want to know something? D'you know when I wanted you the most?

— I can't imagine.

— When we fought … you know, before Hector went away. I thought you were magnificent. I couldn't work out why we hadn't done it before, got all the bad stuff out in the open. I wanted to come up that night, break down the door and ravage you. Sorry, but it's the truth.

— You've been drinking, Ronnie.

He was now lying on the covers, stroking my neck.

— Sometimes drink brings out the truth.

I looked at him, at his warm eyes, his still somehow inviting skin. With drink, he lacked the guile of the day-to-day Ronnie, so that all that was left was a quite charming, if tipsy, middle-aged man.

— I don't want to be hurt again, Ronnie.

— You won't be, ever, I swear.

— I wish I could believe you.

— That's all finished. I was a fool, I know I was, but I've changed. And apart from being even more beautiful, so have you, I think.

He had a tenacity at such moments lacking in all the other aspects of his life.

— You are beautiful, he murmured, baring my shoulders and kissing them. — So bloody lovely.

CHAPTER EIGHT

1963

It was a time of change. Factories were built outside Monument, people acquired cars and houses began to appear on recently green fields, almost as far as the holy well on Captain Penny's Road. When Hector stepped from the boat at Easter, it took me a moment to recognise him, six feet tall and twice as broad as I remembered. I saw girls on the wharf suck in their breaths.

— Hector!

He smiled and hugged me.

—You're enormous!

— I'm ravenous.

— Your old mother had reckoned as much. Let's go home.

We drove out Captain Penny's Road and took the fork for Sibrille. The grass had that glistening, April newness. In some places, milk herds had just been let out after their winter's confinement and, muddied and shed stained, bucked their way across green meadows.

— How's Dad?

— He's at work.

— Is it going well?

— I'm not told.

— You said in your letter that there were some problems.

— There are always problems, Hector, I said as we breasted the last hill. We shouted together, — *I see the sea!*

I liked to stand and watch him as he ate, in silence, a serious business.

— So good. God, I was starving. He leaned back, hands clasped. — You're looking well, Mum.

— You should go and see your grandfather.

— I'll see him when we go to Mass tomorrow.

— He doesn't go any more, Hector. The priest comes once a month with Communion.

Hector made a surprised face. — How's Stonely?

— I'll tell you something funny. A man rang their doorbell last week checking for dog licences and Delaney answered it just as Stonely appeared around the side of the house. 'What do you want?' Stonely asked him. 'It's all right, sir,' the man said, 'your wife can look after me.'

Hector chuckled and took from his pocket a box of cigarettes and offered me one.

— No, thanks.

— You don't mind if I do?

— Not at all.

— All the emphasis in school is on what we do when we leave next year, said Hector, puffing. — I've been talking to the careers bloke. Got on well with him. He's given me lots to think about.

— Oh?

I had not prepared well for this moment, for although I could not bear to think of Hector coming back here and launching into a business career with Ronnie – something Ronnie had more than once alluded to – neither could I bear the thought of him going away.

— I think I'm going to join the army, Hector said.

— Hector?

— Royal Green Jackets, Rifle Brigade, Granddad's old regiment.

My breath lost its rhythm.

— Chap in school has all the details. First I go to an officer's training college, which is a bit like a university, then the world's my oyster. See places like Australia, Belize, Hong Kong. I'll be an officer.

I could not deal with all the cascading images.

— That's … wonderful. But you have another year before you make your mind up.

— I think I have made my mind up, Mum.

We all walked out the causeway that evening, to the drowned soldiers' plaque, and watched the boats coming in on the tide.

Ronnie said, — Beware the army. Pay you nothing, lure you in with cheap talk about faraway places, then throw you on the scrapheap when you're thirty.

—Your father's right, Hector, I said, swept by unexpected relief for Ronnie's opinion.

— Different in my day, Ronnie went on, there was a war. And an empire. Stay at home, is my advice.

— With respect, there's not an awful lot here … I mean, in Ireland, said Hector, suddenly pale.

— They say this Common Market will lift all the boats, Ronnie said.

— Do you think England will go in with a lot of Germans? Hector asked.

— Maybe not, but Ireland can't wait, and if we do, the money will all be for farmers. Think of what that will do to land. You could see farms going for five, six hundred pounds an acre.

— You'll make a fortune, Dad.

— And you can be here helping me to make it. A lot better than getting your head blown off by some bloody fanatic.

They fished almost every day of that holiday, on the Thom in Main, from a boat off Sibrille and from the rocks outside our back door. I saw the ease in Ronnie, the untroubled slope of his shoulders as he walked side by side with Hector, their waders clomping. For those parts of the day when Ronnie had to go into Monument and I had Hector to myself, we chatted of other times in Sibrille, of Peppy, whom Hector had never really known, and of life's enduring imperfections.

— Mum, were you ever in love before?

— Before?

Hector was staring, as if my face had revealed something new of me.

— Before Dad.

— Why do you ask?

— I bet you were, weren't you?

— Oh, maybe I thought I was.

— Who was he?

— Just someone.

— We never talk about your family, Hector said. — I found an old photograph once, you when you were young with two women, one of them old and wearing a black straw hat.

— Oh. My mother and my sister, I said, and the day of that photo pierced me. — We had fifteen hundred acres.

— Gosh. What happened to it?

— It went the same way as Gortbeg in the end. It was seized and redistributed.

— What a shame.

— Actually, I think it was a good thing.

— Imagine what Dad would do now if he could get his hands on fifteen hundred acres. By the way, I've asked Lucy Toms to come to supper tonight, is that all right?

— Lucy? How old is she?

— She's sixteen, Hector said and laughed. — She's fun. She's already had half a dozen boyfriends, according to Dad.

— The last time I saw her she was in a pram, I said.

— I'm going to tell her that, Hector said.

❧

Lucy Toms had dyed her hair bright red and she chain smoked. The afterthought of aged parents – her mother had been over fifty; Lucy's birth had killed her, they said – she had, without discussion, left the girls' school she had been sent to in Monument and lived, it seemed, beyond anyone's control or censure. She was most attractive. I had cooked pork loin, Hector's favourite meal, and had gone into town and bought a bottle of red wine for the occasion. After supper, the three of us went up and sat in the lantern bay. Ronnie had sent word that he would not be home until after ten: he was in Deilt closing a sale, a procedure that apparently involved drinking whiskey.

— I've always wanted to live here, Lucy said drowsily. — My idea of heaven.

Hector, somewhat glassy eyed from the wine, sat in awe of such sophistication.

— You live in a lovely house, Lucy, I said, for she did, albeit one that was crumbling, one of the few Georgian houses on this side of Monument and still standing on more than four hundred acres.

— I hate it, Lucy said.

Her legs were crossed and the shape of her thighs stood out through her thin cotton skirt.

— Why? I asked.

— I just do. I hate it.

— Your father was born there. He's worked very hard all his life to maintain it.

— That's why I hate it. It's made him half mad.

— How is your sister?

— Poor Bibs. The girl leaned back, her eyes closed, and blew perfect smoke rings from her perfect mouth. — She's moved to Dublin, there're more men there.

— I hadn't realised she'd gone.

— Went the week after Christmas. She doesn't even write any more. Lucy's gaze lacked even a hint of warmth. She smiled. — I wanted her to stay at home and marry Beasley.

— Who's Beasley?

Lucy giggled. — Chap in the yard. Hair my colour, and a beard. Looks a bit like Jesus Christ. Strong as a cart horse. She bit her lip. — And twice as dense.

Hector's head went between his knees as he tried to control his laughter.

— One of the women who comes in to wash reported that he has the most enormous … equipment, Lucy said and then, herself, fell silent as she shook with mirth.

I had wondered if I would feel jealous of another woman's attentions for Hector, but all I felt was dismay.

— And why didn't Bibs stay at home and marry Mr Beasley? I enquired, my anger risen from nowhere.

Lucy composed herself. — Bibs would have loved to marry him, but she couldn't because she thought she'd be letting the side down.

— She can't marry Beasley, Mum! Hector said, as if I had missed out on crucial principles.

— I think if you love someone you should marry them, I said, aware that I was giving away too much of myself. — Your life will never be worth living if you don't remember that.

— Then you should have married your mystery man, Hector said.

I felt myself tremble. Hector might have slapped me in the face as said what he had, such a precious thing between us revealed like that in front of a stranger.

— Hector, I chided, making light of it. — That was our secret.

— Did you want to marry him?

— I married your father. Does that answer your question? Now, I think we should have some tea.

— But if you had, said Lucy, smiling, then there'd be some other wifey here in the lighthouse, wouldn't there?

I stood up. — I'm not a wifey, I said and left the room.

CHAPTER NINE

1966

One morning, Stonely collapsed on the causeway. Removed to Monument by ambulance, he died that night. In no worthwhile sense had I ever known him enough to feel grief, but felt instead a sense of loss for the last of Peppy's memories. Photographs had survived of a clutch of blonde-headed children in a garden. Peppy had been about twelve and the brooding child whom she held about the waist must have been Stonely. I wrote to an address in England where, possibly through the female line, relatives lived, grandnephews of Stonely's, or perhaps cousins; I had no idea. No letter came back. It seemed impossible, I wrote to Hector in his officers' training college, that only this photograph remained as evidence that these fair-haired children had ever existed.

Stonely's death had unforeseen consequences for the status quo at the coastguard station. Delaney left.

Inconsolable, she took to her bed and refused to cater. One day men came from Baiscne, kinsmen on whom she had not set eyes for forty-five years, and took her away. She had nothing to say after all that time – whatever ties she'd ever had to the Shaws were frayed beyond repair. She did not even look in on Langley before she left or await Ronnie's return. Langley's nurse refused to cook. Ronnie suggested I fill the gap, but it was more a void than a gap. Seeing myself landed with the role of cook to a paid servant, I too refused. Threatened with starvation, the nurse packed her bags and Langley went into the County Home in Monument.

We were all at once a garrison of two, as Ronnie put it. Or as was more often the case, of one, for he was an early riser and liked the coffee that was to be had in Monument, and on most weekday nights found his meal somewhere along the way. And yet, over time, the sharp edges of conflict seemed to have become somewhat rounded between us, for we behaved as I imagined civilised people did and every Sunday morning, without fail, went up the causeway together and, as custom had evolved, sat in the second pew on the right-hand side of the nave for eleven o'clock Mass. Courteous and charming as a rule, Ronnie was easy to live with. He was forty-eight and I would soon be forty-four. When we spoke, it was mostly about Hector, transferring soon to the British army on the Rhine, and his future in the army, and Ronnie's unaltered view of the opportunities awaiting young men in Ireland's under-worked, undervalued acres. His eyes had become softer with age and, I believed, more seeing of me. I no longer smelled other women on his clothes.

I look back with little regret on that part of my life,

without any measurable yearning that, for example, I should have put time to better use. Every other week I did my shopping in Monument and every other week something changed: the Shortcourse who owned the butchers in Balaklava died; his descendant, a young, local politician, took over and transformed the shop into a place of gleaming steel counters staffed by butchers who wore pork-pie hats; Ronnie attended the huge funeral of a Mrs Bensey, formerly Church, a family that owned more land in Monument than the Harbour Commissioners.

I was a creature of Sibrille's seasons. On summer days, I lay on cliffs trimmed with wild flowers, reading a book and marvelling at the vastness of the sea. I watched the same sea rise in autumn and its colour flee, the cliffs becoming distant, inaccessible places while the seabirds spent the shortening days in the lee of jagged outcrops. Sibrille's sixteen hours of winter darkness seemed to cut it off from the outer world and made the people warmer and more caring of one another. Although the night skies were sumptuous, neither the sea nor the land had much to offer during this season, so the farmers and fishermen drew their days in around them by taking a morning to come in and post a letter, or an afternoon to top up their provisions. Even though I now had Langley's old car, I seldom went to Monument outside my fortnightly trips. Instead, I liked to spend an afternoon sitting under a light at the back of the pub in Sibrille, reading for an hour, the sense of closeness, the soft chat about games and fishing boats riding just at the edge of my hearing. From the lantern bay at night, I would catch the homegoings, the engines of cars and tractors. March brought storms. It was then that I missed Hector most, for we had, when he was a child, sat together behind the thick glass and watched the sea try to devour us, had clung together at each new, engulfing eruption and when the froth had run whitely down the windows and we could see far out the approach of the next gigantic onslaught, we had, in one delicious voice, screamed.

∽◌∾

Ronnie came home early, declined food and went to bed. Late August. The summer had been short, all the talk was of ruined crops and the high price of hay.

— There's a letter from Hector, I said the next morning, somewhat surprised to see that he had not already left for work.

— He's well?

— He's being made a first lieutenant.

— Really.

— Maybe he'll be the first Shaw to become, I don't know, what's next – a general? I handed Ronnie the letter.

— He's full of questions about you, how your business is going. You should write to him.

Ronnie picked up the letter. His hand was trembling.

—Yes.

— Is there something the matter?

Ronnie gulped a breath. — I've left Gargan.

—You've … left?

—We have parted company.

— Is there a good reason?

— He's not a nice man. Comes from nothing. Never paid me for all my mileage, the hours I spent finding farmers who would sell. You know how hard I tried. Don't you?

— Of course.

— Some people have no idea how things work, how you have to forage for yourself in this business. Take your chances.

— What have you done, Ronnie?

Ronnie was ashen. — There's a problem with a client.

— How big a problem?

— They may bring charges.

In the weeks that followed it was, I now accept, a reflection of the poverty of our relationship that Ronnie had never seemed more lovable. That he needed to be either invalided or broke or facing prosecution, as it turned out he was, in order for us to be close was the reality. Acting as advisor to an Englishman, he had gone out with this man's trust and money and purchased him a farm of land. Six months later, when the new owner had moved in, the former farmer who still lived in the vicinity had called to wish him luck and, in the way of these things, when drink had been consumed, had alluded to the generous cash amount which the vendor had paid back to Captain Ronald Shaw, MBVI, as part of the deal. The outraged Englishman had arrived one morning into Gargan's office and standing at the front counter with eleven others present, accused Ronnie of being a swindler. Ronnie, he alleged, had acted not in his best interests, but rather had used his trust to pay too much and, in the process, benefited himself. The transaction was fraudulent and the purchaser would now rescind it. The gardaí were informed. The file was sent to Dublin. Ronnie put the coastguard house on the market.

I understood his concern that Hector would not learn of the scandal. He was, in the end, the only one either of us would in our hearts be left with. All at once, Hector's career seemed a blessing, his distance a mercy beyond words and his prospects away from Sibrille, from us, the only hope for the future. Weeks went by, then, in November, Ronnie, with no action against him yet in view, resumed the work of his pre-Gargan days, that is, ferreting out land for sale and finding buyers, but he found it tougher going. No one changes slower than a farmer, but the change, when it comes, is complete. Ronnie's problems were the talk of Monument and the coastguard house was sold for half its worth to people from Kilkenny as a holiday retreat. The money all went to pay debts. The remaining Shaw land outside Sibrille, still in Langley's name and mortgaged to a bank, was disposed of quietly and Ronnie received nothing from the proceeds. When Hector wrote to say that he could not get home leave for Christmas, I felt relief in a way I would never have thought possible.

෧෩

Over the years, I had used the money from the rent of Peppy's house in Dublin to make up our shortage of cash; now, all of a sudden, it was all we had. And yet, in our decline, as a bass from the sea became the difference between a good meal or not, as the lighthouse which needed painting each spring was left peeling and the untended gardens around us reverted at speed to chaos, we had long days together of warmth and easiness, and evenings sitting before the fire, laughing about some old memory to do with Peppy or Langley, wondering where Delaney had got to, or imagining the success Hector was as a soldier. I saw Ronnie send me glances of genuine affection and I wondered if, over the years, had we been cast adrift together even more, as it were, whether we might not have made a better fist of things.

— This can't go on, I said one evening.

Earlier, a most apologetic man had come around and had cut off the telephone.

— We should leave. Begin again.

— How?

— We should sell here and move to Dublin.

He looked at me. — You're serious.

— What's the point of staying? There's a fine house in Dublin. We're not known there. You could get a job – doing something other than auctioneering.

Ronnie's eyes blinked at speed. — It's the only thing I know.

— You weren't an auctioneer in the army.

— That was more than twenty years ago.

— Ronnie, it's no reflection on you, but it hasn't been the greatest success. It's time to rethink, move on. People do it the whole time. A fresh start.

— I've never thought of living anywhere else. It seems … it seems wrong somehow. The fact is, I like living here.

— So do I, Ronnie.

No more was said. The great rush of light in late April and in May seemed to drive our problems before it. Heat grew back into the cliffs. Seabirds hatched and hunted. One morning after rain, the whole coastline was a blaze of colour. Then Ronnie came in very late; it was two, a night of a bright moon and a restless, undulating sea. I heard him go into his room downstairs, for although our sleeping apart was not invariable, we had, I think, both come to like the independence of it.

—You were late, I said the next morning.

Ronnie looked up from pouring tea, his face caught by an old but to me disturbing confidence.

—We may not be dead yet, he said.

— Oh.

He nodded, poured for me. — A farm. A big one. I think I'll get the sale.

—Whose?

— I'd rather not say till it's in the bag.

—Well … that's very good.

— We'll turn the corner here, just you wait and see, Ronnie said and winked.

It was this prospect of success rather than our enduring climate of failure that made my mind up. Apart from the threat of legal action from the Gargan business that had not gone away, we had on countless occasions been here before. Ronnie would get this farm to sell and the commission would come in, and he would begin again to tangle, as they had it in Monument, and spend night and day seducing those with land to sell or with money to buy it, and our problems would be put into suspension until the next crisis came along, except that we would by then be that much older. I didn't say anything to Ronnie, but a week later, on a warm June afternoon, I drove into Monument to meet Dick Coad.

— This place … he said vaguely, waving his hand over the disorder. His father had died some years before and Dick alone now ran the practice. Lifting a stack of files from a chair, he placed them up like sandbags on his already fortified desk. Smoke streamed into his left eye in an endearing recapturing of the past. He had little remaining hair and had become thinner, a development that made him look even more eccentric. Fishing around on his desk, perhaps for some documentation relevant to me, he abandoned the search, removed his cigarette from his mouth and tipped its impending ash into the palm of his left hand.

— Forgive me.

— How are you, Dick?

— I am, thank God, uncommonly well, and if I may say so, if appearances mean anything, so are you, Iz.

I caught in the air between us the merest whiff of alcohol. He said,

— I've just brought out a book, you know. *The History of Monument and District.* Took me all of ten years.

— Oh. And is it under your own name?

— Indeed it is. Richard Coad. It can be found in the library and in the tourist office.

I allowed a small and respectful moment of silence for his achievement.

— Dick, we have decided to move to Dublin.

— Ah.

— Nothing remains here to keep us, really. Our son Hector is in the British army, Ronnie's father is in the County Home and quite demented, poor man, knows no one. It is time for a fresh start.

— So you would ...

— Sell the lighthouse.

— And ...

— Move into my house in Dublin. Which is why I am here, to enquire about what needs to be done in order to make it vacant for us.

— Nothing too arduous, rest assured. Dick flamed another cigarette to life. — Tell me, what regiment did

Hector go into?

— Royal Green Jackets.

— Ah, yes, old Captain Shaw's regiment. They fought at Waterloo, you know. They actually wore green jackets, hence the name. What a grand tradition! Crimea and then the Cape. Old Captain Shaw would not have actually fought — if I tell a lie, forgive me — but I don't believe he ever saw action. But the regimental lore! Inescapable! Light infantry charging cannon side by side with cavalry. Brave horses that could face down fire. Splendid. Many such horses shipped out from around Monument, you know, the progeny of mares owned by small farmers. Massive steeds with hearts as big as buckets. Blood going back to the time of Cúchulainn. The joy of it!

Dick's eyes rolled in their unilateral orbits.

— I would have some concerns about your proposal, Iz.

— Oh?

— Which I would only express in the light of our acquaintance — one I greatly value — and the element of trust I still feel I must discharge on behalf of the late Mrs Shaw, whose memory my late father always retained with great affection, God rest them both.

— Ronnie and I have been through a lot, but we're still together.

— No less than an example to everyone — but who am I to talk, without a wife to my name? Yet the principle of the original bequest remains. How long is it since we went to Dublin that day? Eight years?

— Thirteen.

— Heavens above! Of course, how could you forget, and the circumstances in which you came home? I lit candles that night in Dublin for the child. And for you. Poor

Jennings passed on, you know. Ah yes, fell down dead
during an inspection, poor fellow. He was a gentleman.

— He was. Dick, this is not like selling the house, it is
going to be our home. My home.

— Quite. However, legislation has been passed recently
and there is lots more of it on the go – God knows how
anyone can keep abreast – which complicates questions of
ownership. A wife can no longer be put out on the street,
thank God, on the basis that the house is no longer hers.
Man and wife living in a house confers rights of joint
ownership regardless of whose name is on the deeds. And
thus the same would apply should you move to Dublin. It
is your house now, but were it to become the home of
yourself and Captain Shaw, then it would no longer be your
house in the way Peppy intended.

— Whose house would it be?

— Half of it would be his. Dick's mournful eyes
swivelled. — I'm sorry. You must, of course, be free to live
wheresoever you choose, I'm just like a tiresome old uncle
who has your best interests at heart.

— I'm older than you, I said and laughed.

— Nevertheless.

— What do I do now?

— Think about it and we'll have another chat.

He was a man whose dogged adherence to a principle
was both his greatest asset and what limited him most, for
on the one hand he was right, I thought as I drove home
– the house in Dublin was my safety net; but, then again,
who didn't change over years, and why should Peppy's
bequest be made an obstacle rather than grasped as an
opportunity? Heat burned into the little car. In fields either
side, hay was being turned or ricked or drawn in for the

distant winter. Men worked, sleeves rolled to the elbow, or in some cases they had taken off their shirts so that their torsos looked piebald, milk-white bodies from which sprang nutty forearms and necks. Heat stood over the causeway in undulating veils as I drove in. Ronnie's car was parked around the back of the lighthouse, a surprise, since he had said that morning he would be gone all day.

— Ronnie?

His sports jacket was thrown on the chair in the kitchen.

— Ronnie? Are you up there?

An open window banged somewhere.

— Ronnie?

I climbed the curving stone stairs and yearned for Dublin, a place I knew little of, but where we would at least have some money. The door to his room stood ajar.

— Are you in there?

I walked in and saw the open window through which years ago I had thrown everything he had owned. I stood at it and saw a pink head floating twenty yards out to sea.

— Ronnie!

He turned around.

— Come on in! he cried. — It's magnificent!

❧

They prayed for rain at Mass in Sibrille at the end of June. People spoke of ground like rock, of meadows that had been left too scorched to cut, of crazed cattle stampeding for water. When the rain did come in the first week of July, it washed down the hill of the village, taking weeks of dung and dead flies with it. One day the sea had lain like blue silk, the next it stood rearing, outraged and black as ink. I felt

the opportunity slipping, as if Dick Coad's advice had put
my resolve into a neutral gear so that my common sense
was ebbing. Money was desperately short. Ronnie was
considering signing on the unemployment register in
Monument, an action that would, we knew, cause a
sensation. We had no telephone, the man who had come to
cut off the electricity had been narrowly persuaded to
come back in a week when there would be a cheque and
I had not settled our grocery account in Wise's since the
previous March. And yet Ronnie had an old lift in his gait.
He got his petrol on tick from a variety of places and kept
alluding to the substantial deal he was coaxing along, the
one that would 'set us up'. I hated his deals. I hated his
'foraging', his being out late at night, the distance that came
between us whenever things went well for him and he
didn't need me. In Dublin, he could sign on for welfare
payments and no one would give a damn. He might even
get a job. Dick Coad might be wise in one respect, but in
the main thrust of what I knew was right for us, he had
erred. I got up one morning after Ronnie had left and
drove into Monument in a downpour.

I felt ashamed for not spending more time with Langley
– Ronnie had not been to see him since Christmas – but
the County Home was a grim ordeal for visitors, stinking
as it did of cheap food and bladder. Yet to those like Langley,
clinging with grim determination to three meals a day and
life, it was a home. I passed the gates and prayed that his
merciful release would not be too much longer. Dick Coad
was not in. His sister who sold stationery from the shop
downstairs had no idea where he was.

— Will it ever stop? she asked as we stood in her shop
looking out at the rain.

It was too wet to shop and, anyway, I had no money. With wipers whirring, I drove out on to Long Quay, already under an inch of water. Through a lapping tide, I marvelled at how a town that a week ago had spoken of water rationing now resembled Venice. Short of the Commercial Hotel, a large woman, soaked, was lugging along a heavy suitcase. As I passed, she turned.

— Bibs?

Hair was stuck to Bibs Toms's big cheeks.

— Christ, she said as she got in, I had forgotten quite how hopeless they are in this town.

— What a nice surprise.

— I must have waited at the station for three-quarters of an hour for a taxi that never came.

— I'll bring you home.

Steam rose from Bibs as we met open country and the rain eased.

— This is Langley's old car, isn't it? Is he still …?

— Yes, but he might as well be dead, poor man.

— He was my hero as a child. No one crossed country like old Captain Shaw.

— You must like Dublin. I heard you have a very good job.

— Well, a job. Bibs snorted and squeezed her hair into a queue. — I work in a shop, if you must know. We sell wool.

— I'm sure it's interesting.

— It's dreadful. Then Bibs smiled. — But on Saturday afternoons I take a bus to Rathfarnham and ride out hunters for a businessman.

— So you've two jobs, that's clever.

— Oh, I don't charge him, I just do it for the love.

Exactly halfway to Sibrille was Toms Cross. The right-hand road doubled back for more than two miles before the first acres of the Toms's land was reached.

— We had the best hunt in memory from a meet here, Bibs said. — The fox ran all the way to Eillne, can you believe?

— How often do you come home?

— Not a lot. It's too expensive. Besides, I have my horses in Dublin now.

— Your sister's a pretty girl, I said as the road wound around and the summer hedges began to wetly scrape the windows. — Hector was very taken with her.

— She wrote to say something dreadfully important is happening and that I must come home at once, Bibs said. She shivered. — Hope she hasn't got herself pregnant with that Beasley creature.

— It's a big undertaking for a girl to run a farm on her own. She's very brave, I said as we drove in by gateless piers.

— And looks after Father, another disaster. D'you mind going to the front door? It's less carrying with this damn case.

From the front, the old house appeared uninhabited. The lower windows were shuttered, the paint of the hall door hung in great, drooping tongues and ivy had run amok into the eaves and was threatening the chimneys. Bibs got out and put her suitcase by the boot scrape.

— Come in and have tea.

— I should get home.

— Just for ten minutes, said Bibs and led the way around the side.

We squeezed in past laurel bushes and brought down cupfuls of rain water on ourselves.

— I have such mixed feelings about this house, Bibs was saying. — When I'm away from it, I think about it all the

time, about each room, about the yard and the boxes. I go
to sleep every night remembering every horse that ever
stabled here, even those that were in livery. I smell them. It's
ridiculous.

We had come into a yard at the back.

— And then when I come home, as now, with months
gone by since my last visit, as soon as I arrive the whole
thing begins to take on another appearance. Does that
sound daft? It's as if I've been remembering another place
entirely when I was away, for as soon as I get here I want
to leave again.

She halted and turned to me.

— Do you think I'm completely mad?

I heard her and yet her words held no meaning. Nor did
I see her, for I was staring at the kitchen window of the
farmhouse where her sister Lucy, naked, was braced
forward over the sink, with my husband, Ronnie, behind
her.

CHAPTER TEN

1969

For the first six months, each time I looked out of the bay window and saw a sky of racing clouds, my eyes, by reflex, sought the sea. The silence too I found eerie, especially at night. I had not realised how much a part of me the ever-soughing sea had become, how the blunt crash of water on rock had become so essential. The sound of wind through trees was altogether different, sibilant, light breezes rinsing through the Dublin suburbs and leaving in their aftermath vales of stillness.

I had written and told Hector everything. He had not replied for nearly a month, a delay I found unbearable, and I waited every day for his reply as if for an imprimatur. I had letters from Rosa Santry keeping me up to date with the Monument gossip, but I found the trivia essential to living in a community irrelevant and tiresome once one had left. I awoke one night, startled, and sat up drenched in sweat. I had had a dream, and although it was already fading, some vivid images remained: dead men in cloaks, blood in their nostrils, a copse surrounded by a waist-high wall of large, uneven stones that incorporated a fairy mound where oak trees grew at eccentric angles.

When Hector's letter arrived at last – he had been on manoeuvres – it seemed almost flippant and assumed that the separation was temporary, for he asked whether if he came home for Christmas I would be back in Sibrille by then. I replied, explaining the now-legal nature of affairs, and how I had wanted nothing except my freedom. Although I did not say so to Hector, I realised that what freedom meant was that I would be living on my own from then on and be like the many women forced to refashion their lives from the unfriendly starting point of middle age. Ronnie, on the other hand, planned never to be alone. I learned from Bibs Toms that Lucy had put her father into the County Home, sold the farm and moved into the lighthouse. Ronnie had turned the corner.

I lived on remarkably little. With the help of my lovely Dick Coad, I made a flat in the garden basement and secured a tenant. My new circumstances, in which money was not a constant, unspoken problem, made me realise how insecure we had been in Sibrille and how that state of affairs, created and sustained by Ronnie, had contributed to my mute acquiescence. I joined the Royal Dublin Society where, thirty years before, my father, then a member, had brought me to the Spring Show. One or two people still spoke of him.

Hector's letter in the summer was a sprawling half a dozen pages. It appeared he had come to Ireland and gone to Sibrille unannounced – to me a hurtful piece of information – and discovered Lucy. It had, by his own admission, been an ugly scene. Things broken, Lucy screaming and driving away, Ronnie putting Hector out at the point of a shotgun. Hector had walked to Monument, where he had booked into the Commercial Hotel and, he wrote, for two days had gone on a bad bender. Ronnie had come into town, but Hector had refused to see him. Nor did he want to face coming to see me in Dublin, so ashamed was he of everything that had taken place. I read a new maturity in the letter. He said he never again wanted to meet Ronnie and asked me to come to England. My reaction was mixed. Absurd as it would be for me to be pleading Ronnie's case, neither would I try to prosper in Hector's affections by damning him. Not that I had anything but contempt for my husband; rather, I wanted to spare my son the debilitating environment of hate. So I spent several days over my reply, attempting to achieve a balance and hoping that in Hector's new wisdom, I would find the consolation for which I ached. But before my letter could be posted, word came from Dick Coad in Monument to say that Langley Shaw was dead.

᭠᭠᭠

We drove south in late August sunshine in a car rented by Hector at Dublin Airport. I had brought a picnic basket and we stopped along the coast at a place where wooden benches overlooked the flat Irish Sea.

— How are you coping? he asked.

We both had the same green eyes, but Hector's had been newly wrought by a process of pain.

— Better. No problems about money, for one thing. And

life is always better when something nasty has been confronted.

—You look well.

— Thank you, Hector.

— Have you … is there …

— No, there is no one.

— I'm sorry. I just wanted you to know that if there was, I shouldn't mind.

— That is very sweet of you.

I took his hand and warmed my cheek with it. He had filled out into a man and his hair was cut short except for a quiff at the front that fell over his forehead. I looked at his big hands and wondered what kind of a woman he would find.

— What about you? They must all be swooning over you.

— Nothing too serious, Mother, don't worry.

— I won't. I'm sure she'll be lovely.

— She'll be like you.

— Oh, Hector, that's kind, but you mustn't waste your life looking for a younger me. It's not worth it.

— I have to make that decision.

As the peak of Dollan came into view, he asked, — Are you going to speak to him?

— I shall sympathise with him.

— I shan't. I think he has let us down in a way that is beyond forgiveness.

— I find that concept difficult, Hector.

He pulled in at one of the bends in the foothills as the town appeared all at once below us.

—You could have left him, couldn't you?

—What do you mean?

—You were in love with someone else, that doctor who came from England after Ronnie's accident.

—You mean Hedley Raven? Where on earth did you get that idea?

— Rosa Santry told me.

— Rosa Santry?

Hector covered my hand with his.

—When I was in Monument last year, Rosa came in to see me. Dick Coad asked her to, I think. They thought I was going to top myself or something. Beautiful woman. She told me that years ago she saw you and this English doctor together on the riverbanks in Main. She said you were in love.

I could not stem my tears, nor even protest innocence. — I didn't know she saw us.

— As long as it wasn't my fault.

— How could it possibly have been your fault?

—You probably thought you had to stay with Ronnie on account of me.

Shame rose within me like a monster. — Hector, he meant nothing. Believe me, he was nothing at all.

Hector had reserved two rooms in the Commercial. It seemed eerie being in lodgings once again in a town I had come to know so well. Before supper, I went for a walk down Long Quay. Attended by swarms of seagulls, trawlers were discharging their boxes of catch. Farther down the wharf, a ship was taking on lumber as members of her crew, their eyes white in their dark faces, leaned over the deck rails and smoked cigarettes. I thought, for all its size, how much more tame Dublin was than Monument, how in Dublin one lived in settled, leafy suburbs untouched by commerce or the smell of fish or foreign tobacco. Hector, because of everything that had happened, because of how he now saw Ronnie, would never come to live here, might never, in fact, come back here again. For both our sakes, I had hoped he might return: for his own, because I valued Monument so dearly on his behalf; and for mine because I had imagined myself coming down to visit him. He was in the bar reading the evening paper when I came back in. The front page showed that Ulster was on fire: buses and cars alight, riots in the cities.

— There's talk of us being sent, you know, he said as we sat down either side of an upright plastic menu wedged in a block of wood. — To keep both sides apart.

I felt myself go dizzy. — I'd prefer if you didn't.

Hector smiled at me kindly. — It's part of my job, Mother.

I had not ever thought of this, but now it seemed grotesque.

Hector was saying, — It may all fizzle out. We may not be sent at all. God, I'm hungry. D'you think their steak is any good?

There and then, I wanted to tell him what I had sworn I never would, but I needed time to think and to prepare myself.

Hector was saying, — You like it down here, don't you? Do you have to live in Dublin? I mean, just because that's where you own a house?

— I think by living in Dublin I can love Monument best.

— I'll never live here, he said. — Not because I'm afraid of bumping into Ronnie – I couldn't care less, to be frank – but, and this sounds odd, I've never felt I belong here.

— What do you mean?

— It's an inner thing. I feel more at home in England

than in Ireland, and that's being honest.

— You do belong here, Hector, believe me, I said. — Monument is where you belong.

Langley had been brought to Sibrille's church and the next morning we got there early to put our flowers on his coffin. Local people stood outside the church door and removed their hats when they saw me. My nostrils were met by the smell of candle wax as we walked in and the heels of our shoes echoed in the empty church.

— Mrs Shaw?

A small, hunched man holding a bowler hat at his chest stepped from the shadows. I recognised him as the undertaker from Peppy's funeral.

— You're welcome home, Ma'am. Would you like to see the captain?

For a moment, the meaning of his words confused me. Then I grasped what he was asking.

— Oh, you mean Langley. Hector, he's asking do we want the coffin opened.

Hector drew in his breath. — Why not?

The man removed wreaths from the lid and placed them around the bier, then with quick, knowing fingers went to screws along the side and gently lifted off the top. I stared.

— Isn't he the real old captain? The real McCoy, the undertaker said.

Langley was dressed in hunting pink, complete with neck stock, britches and gleaming black boots with the brown top cuffs of a master of foxhounds. In one yellowing hand was clasped his riding crop; in the other, his hunting horn. Above all this splendour presided his head, midway to the skeletal, but touched up with foundation and rouge so that no resemblance whatsoever to Langley Shaw remained.

— Good Lord, Hector said.

— Whose idea was it? I asked.

— Captain Shaw's idea, Ma'am. I mean, your … his son's idea. To send him off in style the way he liked.

— Could you not have put a horse in too? Hector asked.

We settled on the left of the central aisle, one pew from the front. Very quickly, the little church filled as people came to the coffin and genuflected and placed down their flowers. Langley might not have lived here in over ten years, nor hunted this country in thirty, but the respect he was due for his exploits shone from the faces of the country-men and women who had come to bury him. Nor was his ancient magnanimity to the Catholic Church forgotten, judging by the numbers of priests making their way, satchels in hand, through the alter rails to the sacristy. Father O'Dea, now a parish priest in Monument, paused and shook our hands.

— The end of an era, or maybe not, he said and winked at Hector. — I don't think I'd bother hunting if there wasn't a Shaw to show me the way.

We sat there at the front, unable to turn in our seats and inspect the whispering congregation. Then, as if a blade had fallen, the murmuring ceased. I could hear nothing. Hector was seated forward, elbows on his knees, head in his hands. It was a sliding noise at first, imperceptible unless you listened for it. I strained my eyes into the very corners of their sockets. My husband, alone, had arrived level with our pew. It was Ronnie, beyond a doubt, yet it was Ronnie with twenty years added. He stood, looking down at us.

Then, he genuflected, a most laborious business, and took his place in the foremost pew on the aisle's other side.

I remember little of the service or of the eulogies, hunting stories and prayers. Three teams each of six men from the locality shared the shouldering of Langley out into a day of blissful sunshine, of high swallows, of warm air tinged with the ozone from the nearby sea. When he was lowered down, the huntsman sounded the 'gone away!', shrill pips that stirred the blood, and then the long, mournful notes that draw in the close of the hunting day.

— Ronnie.

He turned to me.

— I just wanted you to know that I am very sorry for your grief. I feel for you.

— Thank you, Iz.

He was looking over my shoulder to where Hector had been a moment before.

— Will you and Hector come back to the pub for a drink? I've arranged food.

— I think not, Ronnie.

— Iz, can we not ... things are not good.

— I'm sorry to hear it.

— I've been a fool.

I couldn't hurt him beside his father's open grave.

— Ronnie, we are what we are. It's not our fault. Don't torture yourself, not today.

— Hector ...

— He's upset, Ronnie.

— He's my son.

— He's upset and angry.

— Oh, God. Come back for ten minutes.

I thought of Hector waiting. — Sorry, I have to go now.

—You don't have to go, Iz.

—Yes, I do.

I felt a wonderful freedom all at once, for I was no longer tied there. I had escaped and could leave without constraint or conscience. Even the sea could not keep me, much as I had once thought it could, for now I ached for the trees in my Dublin garden, the silence at night, the faces of strangers and the balm of solitude. I found Hector by the car.

— Do you want to go to the pub? he asked. — I can drive you there, but I won't go in.

— I want to go home. Now.

It was not until we were coming in along Captain Penny's Road that either of us spoke.

— He looks like death, I said.

— She's left him.

— I don't believe it.

— A couple of months ago. Dick Coad told me.

—Was Dick there?

— He was looking for you. He told me she's run off to England with some old farm hand.

I looked at Hector. — Not Beasley?

— Dick didn't say.

To laugh seemed the only response. — Oh, God, wait till Bibs hears. Poor Ronnie. What a fool.

— He's up to his neck, according to Dick. Some old case in which he diddled someone. They're taking him to court.

—That happened years ago!

— Dick said he could do jail, Hector said and slammed through the gears of the rented car. — And you ask me whether I'd like to come back here again? And be the son of a man who left his wife to live with a tart and who's now all but in the clink because he's a crook? Christ, I never want to set foot in this bloody place again.

As we met the foothills, I thought of how, had it not been for Hector, I might well have gone back for ten minutes, and then learned that Lucy was gone, and of the old trouble that now seemed set to put paid to Ronnie once and for all; and if I had, and had come within reach again of the sea, perhaps I might have thought my freedom to be an illusion and, once again, persuaded myself that my place was with a man who needed me.

CHAPTER ELEVEN

1970

Very slowly, I grew into the daily life of Dublin. The people had a quickness and agility to them, an eye for the main chance but a ready sense of humour that was different to the more open, easy-going inhabitants of a village like Sibrille. Yet Dublin was an amalgamation of little villages, being quite rapidly subsumed into a sprawling conurbation. I went to the cinema one week, to the theatre the next, and struck up polite friendships with the women of my own age who lived in that part of Ballsbridge. I learned bridge and found myself looking forward to our weekly tournaments.

One morning, about a year after Langley's funeral, Rosa Santry rang. Like myself, Rosa was a solitary person and her days were spent in the Santry estate at Main. We spoke about her son, Kevin, who was going to be a solicitor, and about Hector, still with his regiment in Germany and now a captain.

— A real Shaw, Rosa said.

I smiled, a private smile.

— Iz, Ronnie's not well, Rosa said.

— Oh.

— It's this wretched case. Jack says he's gone to nothing.

— I no longer live with Ronnie.

— We just thought you should know.

— He is alone now because he has so chosen. What exactly does Jack mean?

— That he's very thin, neglects his appearance. One would have to be concerned.

— I am concerned. But over the past twenty odd years, every time there has been a crisis in Ronnie's life he has used me to get over it and then, when everything's all right again, he's resumed his old ways. Anyway, we're in the middle of a legal separation. If I become involved with him, he's quite likely to use it against me.

— We thought you should know, said Rosa.

Nevertheless, I rang Dick Coad. He told me of the impending case for fraud, as good as proven by all accounts, in which Ronnie, were he lucky, would have to sell the lighthouse in order to compensate his former client or, at the other end of the scale of fortune, would go to jail for a year or eighteen months. I asked why Ronnie didn't settle ahead of the action so that the case could be withdrawn.

— I understand that Beagles have implored him to, but, apparently, he does not respond, Dick said.

— Should I come down?

A long pause reminded me of the meetings in the cramped upstairs office, reached by a winding stairs redolent of paper since the stocks for the stationery shop were heaped at the inner edges of the risers, and Dick's desk of files and overflowing ashtrays, and the way, at that moment no doubt, his eyes were executing their separate patrols.

— It is entirely up to you, of course, but I do not personally recommend it.

A week later, I received a letter, the postmark Monument. The writing had been executed with a pen whose nib made gothic sweeps and curves of each letter.

Dear Mrs Shaw

I write only because I know you to be a person of great compassion who has herself, over a lifetime, known much pain and suffering.

I have always admired you, from the early days when the hounds met in Sibrille and you came out on foot. I look back on those good days, as I'm sure you do, and wonder how life could have changed so much, almost without our knowing it.

I know you are aware that things have gone downhill in a big way for the poor Captain. I am also aware, of course, of your legal position and have hesitated greatly before putting pen to paper. Saint Paul once said in a letter to the Romans: 'We then that are strong ought to bear the infirmities of the weak.' I think his words have given me courage to write to you. If you are strong enough now, then there is someone very weak who needs you to bear his infirmities.

I won't say more, other than that you are both in my daily prayers.

Most sincerely,

Jack O'Dea (Father) PP

P.S. Please give my best wishes to Hector when you see him. JO'D.

I walked in a park of swishing poplars, now in their autumn yellows, and felt the rain in my face, took off my scarf to let the weather at my hair and watched crows wheeling against the gathering dusk. I was being asked to go back in order to rescue Ronnie from the grave he had dug himself and now bestrode. The old me, a person of compassion, would have gone. And yet, I wondered if I had it in me to be this new person, denying my saving hand to my husband. I needed to speak to Hector before I made my mind up. There was a number. I went home and found it, but before I could pick up the receiver, the telephone rang.

— Mother, it's me.

— Hector. I was just about to phone you.

— Are you all right?

— Well , yes. It's wonderful to hear from you. Where are you?

— Listen, do you remember when we went down for Langley's funeral, we had a chat and I mentioned a few things?

We had talked about so many things, including Langley and Ronnie and how Hector could never live in Monument. About Hedley Raven. When Hector had returned to England, I had shivered at that memory, still clear but in miniature, as it were, a moment of shame perfectly preserved.

— Of course I remember.

— Have you talked to anyone? I mean, have you discussed what I said?

— We talked about our personal lives, not something I would tell someone else, surely you know that.

— No, I'm talking about what I said about, you know, my job. Where I might be sent.

— You mean the …

— Yes. No names. But yes, that is what I mean.

— Oh. So are you being sent?

— It's all top secret and I'd be in one hell of a stew if anyone thought I'd been jabbering on. But the way things are going there at the moment, it seems likely.

— I'm expecting you home for Christmas. Here. In Dublin.

— Consider it done.

— Do keep safe. Hector?

But he was gone, sucked back to wherever he was in Germany or England and I was left on my own, holding a telephone in Dublin and trying, once again, to come to terms with life's monstrous ironies. And yet, through whatever process had taken place during our conversation, I was now quite resolved that I never wanted to see Ronnie again. Yet, in early November, on a midweek night just as I was about to go to bed, there came a knock on the front door. Had I been downstairs I would have gone directly to it, but as it was I went to the window of my bedroom and looked down. Despite his upturned collar and slouched hat, it could only have been him. He looked even more wretched than he had the last time I had seen him, over a year before. As he glanced up, I withdrew.

— Iz?

I sat, trembling, on my bed. He shouted up.

— Iz, I've come up because we must talk. Iz!

Up to that moment, I had thought I could dip in and out of my past, safe here in my house, but now, all at once, my independence seemed feeble. I was afraid of him.

— Iz! You're up there, I saw you. I want to come in! It's raining!

If I let him in and brought him up and eventually allowed him the warmth of my breast, and over the next six months gave him succour and shelter, he would as sure as

116

the fall of night, when he had done with me, let me down again. I could not take any more wounding.

— I'm going to kick this fucking door down if you don't open it! Do you hear me, Iz?

My hand was steady as I dialled the number. He was kicking now. Shouting. I spoke my name and address.

— Iz! Open this fucking door!

I began to dress. In the mirror of the dressing table, I saw someone of years ago. I had sworn not to torture myself about that, but that night of all nights it came back without remorse.

—You needed me once, Iz, didn't you? Did I let you stay outside with nowhere to go? Did I turn my back on you?

I had seen people in cottages along the cliffs outside Sibrille, women feeding hens and leaning over their half doors, and I had plunged with envy. From the first day I had been driven down in Ronnie's old, squeaky car, I had known that I was staking everything. Although I had lost much in that epic gamble, I had also won. Hector had grown up with a father.

— I'm going to kill myself, Iz.

A car's engine and the sound of heavy shoes on my gravel. Men's voices.

— Come along out of that now!

—Take your fucking hands off me! She's my wife!

Scuffling noises. I heard an empty milk bottle topple over. I was glad Hector was gone from our lives; I was so thankful he was not there to see his father dragged away.

— Iz! *Iz!*

The guards came in wearing their caps and wrote things down, declined tea and promised to bring him to the Monument train the next morning and put him on it. One

117

of them, a man of silver hair, told me that he remembered my mother coming here thirty-five years ago. He meant Peppy.

— I'd see her out there herself gardening. A real lady, you could tell.

I didn't tell him that she was not my mother but the mother of the man he had just arrested.

— I drove her home one day, you know?

I looked at the guard, trying to make sense of his words. He chuckled.

— Oh yes, she couldn't drive, and the man who was sent up from Monument to take her home, a hackney man, had a seizure outside this very house, and they took him away in an ambulance. 'You drive me,' she said, because we'd been called, and begod I did, all the way down to Sibrille in the hackney car and came home in the train.

They went out through my hall with their torches and night sticks, the damp rising in a fine mist from their tunics.

— Ring us, Ma'am, if he ever bothers you again.

— He won't. Please don't hurt him, I said.

∂∾ଙ

Over the couple of weeks that followed I tried to equate my pain with that of childbirth, an inevitable human process that always preceeded freedom and exultation; for however much I rationalised what I had decided or tried to concentrate on Christmas, I could not escape the cruel image of Ronnie dead. All my fears for him were on behalf of Hector, who I knew must still have kept a small place in his heart for the man he had so adored. That understanding decided me, not due to any meanness on my part where Ronnie was concerned, but because it was well past the time when Hector should have been told the truth.

As the days drew in, I hoped Ronnie would have the courage to end his own life rather than have to face the shame of a trial and prison, of impoverishment, of living off the charity of friends like the Santrys, for he would die of sadness from all that anyway; better if it came quick and on his own terms, which was how his life had been lived, however warped. My image was of him in the sea that day he had called out to me, his pink, bobbing head, and now in the sea again, but dead. I would not be hypocritical, I had decided. When the time came, I would not go down to Monument and honour him dead where I had denied him alive.

The late November Dublin streets, although dark and wet, embraced me with a welcome anonymity. As I used to do in Sibrille, I found a pub where I could sit with a book on an afternoon with a pot of tea, on the edge of voices and discussions; the evenings on which there was no bridge to play, I spent either in the RDS library or at home in my bedroom. As the year hurtled towards its nadir, so the lights of the shops grew ever brighter and the fires of the pubs warmer. As December turned, newspapers spoke of more trouble in Belfast, of bombs. On television, soldiers ran under sniper fire. A church burned to the ground. I wondered if Hector, were he posted there in the New Year, could refuse to go.

On the days leading up to December 7th, the burden of Ronnie's fate became almost unbearable. Walking home along Herbert Park, I almost wished him to be hiding in the shadows or sitting in the dark cars parked along the road outside my house. In shops and pubs, I heard his voice, I was sure, or saw his face in a queue waiting for a bus. I could not shake myself free of him. I wished the final news would come so that I could mourn him properly, on my own, and reclaim my life. This impending event led me to wonder how I could have such clear foresight about the end of someone else's life, and whether that was wrong, or if I should or could do anything to save him. Several times I picked up the phone to ring people who might somehow be effective in heading off what was going to happen: Rosa, Dick, Father O'Dea. But then I realised as I replaced the phone, unused, that whatever I achieved by ringing them would be temporary, a mere delay, that the same agony would revisit me at Ronnie's next convulsion, as it always had, and that my life, in the meantime, would remain in limbo.

I tried to focus on Christmas, making lists, constructing dates for Hector and myself. A play. A meal in a good restaurant. Drinks with a few new friends. I walked into Dublin on December 6th in an effort to connect myself with people and events and thus become part of them. Strings of lights crisscrossed Grafton Street. People stood at a large shop window, at one end of which sat a Santa Claus, at the other, rows of new television sets, all on an English station which was showing pictures of someplace in Northern Ireland where a man had been shot by a sniper at a distance of three-quarters of a mile. Reality, although brutal, was welcome, as if I had needed to scuff my hand against something rough in order to wake up. I bought wrapping paper and Christmas cards and went home and slept soundly.

I woke up excited by a decision I had come to overnight: I was going to buy a television set. I wondered what was involved and whether I was in time to have it installed by Christmas. I was putting away the things from breakfast when the doorbell rang. For some self-protective reason, I walked first into the front room and to the bay window from which the hall door could be seen. There stood the silver-haired guard of some weeks before, this time cap beneath his arm, and a tall, grey-faced man in a suit.

My legs became unsteady at the knees, for despite the fact that I had envisaged the moment down to almost this very detail, I had not anticipated its physical effect. I began to cry, for somewhere in Ronnie there had been a person I had loved, but he had remained resolutely hidden for much of our life together. I was glad too for him, as I went into the hall, that it was over at last. My tears, as always, were for what Hector was going to feel, or if he would be able to weep. I would do so for both of us.

— Ah, Mrs Shaw.

He was a kind man with big warm hands. I held on to his arm.

— Where would you like to sit, Ma'am?

I was crying and shaking my head. We sat together, me and the guard, and he held my hands in his.

— So you know, Ma'am?

I nodded. — I've known for weeks.

I saw the guard and the other man exchange glances.

— I can stay here as long as you want, the guard said. — You must have great memories.

I laughed. — Some. Some not so great.

— I know, I know.

— How ... how did ...?

— Instantly, said the other man, pulling over a chair. Something about the way he spoke. He introduced himself, but I heard nothing. He said, — He didn't suffer.

— He's with God now, Ma'am, said the guard. — Hector is with God.

— Ronnie, I said. — Hector is our son.

The men looked at one another.

— Ma'am, said the guard, Hector has been killed in Belfast.

How slow the mind, I often thought in the months after, but how quick the heart. I began to scream, even as I knew what they were telling me was impossible. The other man's voice, English, the words 'military intelligence'. I ran upstairs to my bedroom and locked the door because I thought they were trying to kill me. I screamed. As long as I screamed, I could not hear.

I can't say how it came about, but the evening of that day arrived without time intervening. My house was so filled with old friends that I thought I was back in Monument. Dick Coad, Father O'Dea. The Santrys. Bibs Toms. And neighbours from the other houses in the road who brought food and a chaplain of some sort who seemed to be connected with the British army, who sat trying to get it through to me: he spoke of intelligence, of heroes and cowards. Of Hector's background, which was why he had volunteered for military intelligence. The first British officer to be murdered in Ulster.

History had been stood upside down and hung there, gloating. The faces of dead men, blood on their lips and in their nostrils, and a game played on a huge expanse, assailed me.

— I've lost him, I said.

Rosa held my hands in hers. She was warm and kind.

— You must find him, Iz. You must bring him back.

People came and went continuously and my head was spinning. And then Father O'Dea, gently, my sorrow in his eyes, said, — Iz, love, poor Ronnie's here.

That day saw the second great hinging of my life. As they led him in, I could see the truth of the saying that no matter how wretched you are, there is someone, somewhere, even less fortunate. For there were men far more despicable in the world than Ronnie Shaw, but few more pitiful.

— I had nowhere else to go.

— I know, Ronnie.

He knelt at my feet and wept, his sobs unending, as if all that was in him must try and leave him by his eyes. He made me calm. He looked at me now and then from the face of a stranger, not an outsider, just someone I had not seen before. Even as the shadows of evening stole from the open door to the hall across the living room and the people from the nearby houses began to go home and the murmurings from all over the house ceased, Ronnie cried. I kept thinking how sad it would be for Hector to see his father like this. It was Dick Coad who helped him up, at last, and brought him out and down the front steps and put him in a car to drive him home to Monument.

Dick Coad sat back from his desk, his memory racing. The journey home from Dublin on the day after Hector's death had been the loneliest of his life. He had not believed before that he could love her more than he already did. He had been wrong. If he had only had the courage when she had moved to Dublin to follow her, to attend to her every need, to be the friend she relied on most – the thought had pursued him for years. To give her love. 'My lovely Dick Coad.' The image of the years that they might then have had together seared Dick. What had held him back? Lack of nerve, granted. But was there not something more? Fear of what he did not know?

Dick looked at the second package on his desk. Down on the quayside, out of sight, the hooter of the mud dredger sounded. He had heard the rumours over the early years, of course, the whole town had been alive with them, could speak of little else. Many seemed to think her coming to live in Sibrille – almost amongst them, as it were – was brazen and outrageous. Except for her shopping trips, she was rarely seen, had few friends. It was as if, even at twenty-three, she had lived most of her life before she ever came to Monument. Something she never spoke of, nor indeed had Ronnie, although he must have known.

Picking up the paperknife, Dick slit the wrapping paper.

2

Iz

CHAPTER TWELVE

1943

She came towards me, part of the sunlight, her rich, wavy hair covering her shoulders, and I wondered how anyone could be so beautiful. I was in awe of her. So was everyone in Longstead.

— Iz? You've ... done something! She stood Bill, the old horse she rode, on the gravel drive. — What have you done?

— Do you like it?

— Oh, God, you've cut it all off! Bella cried. — Turn around!

I saw my reflection in the French windows as I turned. The sun felt hot on my newly bared neck.

— You look like a boy! Bella cried as she trotted the horse away in precise crunches. — My sister is a boy!

She would be twenty-three that August and had come home from London for her party. I was twenty-one. I'd cut my hair short the week before when I'd lain upstairs in bed, drenched in sweat, shivering with a fever. My mother, Violet, made me recite lists to calm my swirling head. The prime ministers of England, the kings and queens, Dublin streets with churches. Bus numbers, characters from Shakespeare.

— I used to marshal lists like soldiers when I was a child, she told me. — Had it not been for lists, I would have lost my mind.

When my fever broke, my voice had changed. My mother said I sounded like the breeze that blew in March across the lake at Longstead.

☙❧

I knew that Bella's party would be our last as a family, since it was most unlikely that our father would live until my turn came; on the other hand, one never knew. Daddy had been poorly for as long as I could remember. A fall from a horse in his twenties, an undiagnosed ruptured lung, and now his heart. Mother had him carried everywhere since he seldom had the energy to walk. But he had once been young and well and had made the money to buy Longstead from trading in corn. He could still be witty and often retold the times of his encounters with farmers and shippers in Canada and the American Midwest and of the vast potential of Australia, where he had once tended sheep on horseback. Despite his illness, I could now and then catch glimpses of the younger man, a charming companion, a person of intelligence and ambition who had seen much of the world and had loved it.

However, by the time I reached twenty-one, all his

business interests had been sold or had otherwise drained away. My brother, Harry, worked in England for a shipping broker, and Allan, the only one interested in farming, had joined the British army in 1939. Outside our walls, one heard of similar estates as ours being taken over by the Land Commission and carved up between the local farmers who were agitating for more ground. Only the thriving estates would survive, I had heard it said, and the truth was that Longstead, like my father, was slowly dying. Our land was worked out, our ditches blocked, our fences untended and in our once-rich meadows lay the rotted hay of former seasons.

శ్ర‌శ్ర

My mother drove the Ford Victoria down the avenue and onto the public road, which our beeches overhung for a mile. I puffed alight her cigarette and delivered it over, then lit one for myself.

— Did I remember to tell Mrs Rainbow that Daddy would like her bean soup at one?

—Yes, you did.

— I'm losing my mind. I don't remember.

Regardless of season, Mother always went about in old corduroy trousers, flannel shirts, thick pullovers and a hat. She had grown up in the Yorkshire Dales which, she told me, she missed a little every day. From a distance, she looked like a scarecrow.

—You told her, Mother.

— My poor head. Last night I had to get up twice and go downstairs to make sure all the lights had been put out.

Every day, she worked with watercolours; anything that

took her from her easel did so with pain. In a horse-drawn trap, she set out as soon after breakfast as she could, and, during the summer, often did not come back until supper-time. On the very worst of midwinter days, she withdrew to the summerhouse and stayed there until her fingers went numb.

— No one but me ever thinks of these things. Then we get the bills and must pay for everyone's forgetfulness.

— Are we very short of money?

— We are drifting, Iz.

— Perhaps I should get a job.

— Perhaps we all should.

My mother sounded the horn and swerved around a cartload of hay being drawn by a horse.

— Until Allan comes home and takes things in hand, we shall continue to drift. Like a ship without a captain.

— What if he decides not to come home?

Mother's reply was emphatic. — Allan will come home. He'll come home for his horses and his fishing.

— But what if he doesn't?

She looked at me. Her hat, one of black straw, was fixed by a gigantic silver pin.

— Then Bella or you will have to find a suitable husband.

I burst out laughing. — What a thing to say!

— I was married at nineteen.

We pulled in by the grocery store in Tirmon village.

— When I marry it will be for love, I said.

Mr Rafter's shop supplied Longstead with all its needs. These included the food which we did not ourselves produce, our drink, although we drank modestly, feed for horses and cattle, rubber boots, thick socks, flannel shirts, jackets, raincoats, curtain material, bed sheets and pillow cases and all the accoutrements needed to keep a fifteen-hundred acre enterprise, however faltering, on the go. Except for Sundays, no day went by without a transaction with Mr Rafter. He, in turn, played the central role in the sale of Longstead's beef, lamb and mutton, hay and milk. In a small room at home between the servants' hall and the main staircase, my father and Mr Rafter spent hours together every other month, following which Mr Rafter would emerge, his hands held in fists at the level of his waistcoat, and say to whosoever of us was there to see him out, — I see a definite improvement.

If money ever changed hands, I was not aware of it.

My mother regarded Mr Rafter's premises as an extension of Longstead; Mr Rafter always managed to be there to open the door when Mother arrived and to take her list.

— Mr Rafter.

— Good morning, Mrs Seston. Miss.

The grocer's eyes were upcurved and naturally conspiratorial. In his mid-fifties, shaped like a sack of grain and with dark hair receding from a shining tan scalp, Mr Rafter was identified with party politics.

— How's Mr Seston?

— In good form, thank you, although he worries about the war.

— War or no war, it's not a bad time of the year if he could get out, although there was a breeze yesterday that would cut the backbone off you.

His words floated behind Mother's inbound steps. Men in brown dustcoats attended behind counters as we forged through the sudden collision of aromas in the elongated shop. Smoked ham gave way to coffee which yielded in turn to timber, polish, rope, cured lamb fleece, rubber.

— Mr Rafter, we are having some people in. Mother would never use the word 'party'. — Here is the list. We require champagne.

— Certainly.

— And candles. Have I written down candles? I'm losing my mind these days.

Mr Rafter consulted the scrap of paper which Mother had taken all of two minutes to draw up before we had left.

— I don't see … The grocer frowned, slow to be the one to suggest an omission. — How many candles might be required?

— I haven't the faintest idea, I simply remember the last occasion, before the electricity, Lolo's birthday. Every room must have needed two dozen. How many rooms are there? Iz! Do I have to do this *completely* on my own?

This was the first I had heard of candles. I made a rough calculation.

— I'll put down for a gross of the good ones, just to be sure, said Mr Rafter, writing with a pencil into a reassuringly permanent order book.

Mother was pulling vaguely at the corners of a bolt of cloth.

— Italian, silk and wool. The Pope himself has his shirts made from it. Fifteen shillings a yard, Ma'am, said Mr Rafter.

I could see Mother's interest retreat before the price. Too much money, although money was something she never discussed with Mr Rafter. She looked at him as if he had said something that had puzzled her.

— We need bunting, she said.

— Bunting, Mr Rafter repeated, but his pencil remained still.

— In the porch, said Mother.

It was not easy to wrong foot Mr Rafter.

— Coloured paper streamers, I said and Mr Rafter said *Ah* and wrote.

— And huge quantities of bread for sandwiches, Mother said, isn't that all?

She had now reached the rear door to the yard of the premises where oats and meal were stored. Her eyes took in shelves, as if checking for change or movement since her last visit; she turned and at a quickened pace retraced her steps by way of sugar bins and tea chests and labelled drawers piled to the roof.

— And some staff to hand out, as you so kindly provided before, and teapots. As I remember, we must have borrowed them from you or else, if we did buy them, then we've lost them, which I would imagine is impossible, you can't lose twenty teapots, although nothing would surprise me any more.

She halted.

— You arranged the band, Mr Rafter.

— Indeed I did, Ma'am. I collected them off the train myself.

— Are they still …?

— Going strong. I seem to remember they were to everyone's satisfaction.

— They seemed perfectly adequate. Very well, if you could please …

— I'll see to it this morning.

We had reached the door where one of the young men in brown coats had leapt forward to hold it open.

— Put down fish paste, Mother said.

— Fish paste, Mr Rafter wrote in solemn fashion. — And the champagne?

— Just make sure it's good.

— Of course, said Mr Rafter, stepping out after us, but will there be much required?

Mother stared at the shopkeeper. Part of her expected Mr Rafter to know the answer to such a question without his having to ask. We did not entertain very often, but when we did, he should have known that it followed an invariable pattern. At the same time, she considered the question as verging on the impertinent and was not prepared to discuss with a grocer outside his shop how many people we were having in or how much champagne they might drink. And finally, I knew – and knew that Mr Rafter also knew – that Mother had not until that moment attempted to work out how many people might, in fact, be coming to Bella's party.

— Sufficient, Mr Rafter, she said and swept towards our car, me hurrying behind her.

෨⭒෨

I had been to school in Wales. In a tradition initiated by my sister, Lolo, and continued by Bella, three times a year I had boarded the mail boat and sailed to Holyhead. I was meant to have gone on after school, as Bella had, to Paris and Geneva, where one learned to cook and to be in all ways perfect, but there was a war and so I had attended an academy for those purposes in Dublin. My brothers too had been to a minor English public school, with the result, probably intended, that none of us knew very many of the local people around Tirmon, as if Tirmon was not the place we lived but merely dropped into during holidays. This structured aloofness bound Anglo-Irish society to itself; by necessity we reached to the far corners of Ireland for our friends, as if we Anglo-Irish were all related by virtue of ascendancy, intermarriage and religion, and above all by our resolute non-Irishness. If any one thing defined us, that was it. We knew what we were not, and every action and attitude flowed from this fact. We had suffered the onset of Irish independence by, in the main, ignoring it. That we no longer controlled the country in which we lived or that we had been allowed up to now to continue as before seemed to have occurred to no one. We were, of course, not English either, a more awkward truth. The native Irish had only us to go on as an example of Englishness and we gave full value for money in playing the part; but when we went to England or to Wales, we understood that to the English or the Welsh we were Irish. We were, in fact, part of a new race, born of successive plantations from the Middle Ages, but a race that had, by even the most modest standards, failed. We had failed to keep the land we had been sent to settle. Failed to find a way of living with the people we had been sent to rule.

&∘⊱

On the morning of the big day, Mother, having seen my father installed in the morning room, took her easel, palette and paints and disappeared in her pony trap. She would not return, I knew, until evening, for like a child that closes its eyes to hide from monsters, once out of sight of all the bustle and preparation, she would feel safe. Harry, who had come home the day before, was outside, helping to haul up a tent, as Mr Rafter and relays of his men carried in hampers. Harry had always been the one who had made the jokes and livened up the atmosphere at meal times and made Daddy laugh.

— I've never seen so much food, I said.

Bella, in a long dress of cool, baggy sleeves, dragged on her cigarette. She said, — It will all go to the pigs tomorrow, like the last time.

— Better than being stuck for enough.

— Miss Practical. Perhaps you might be practical enough to pour the tea.

We sat in what was called the sunroom, a lean-to at the gable of the house, whose sun was about to be blotted out by the rising tent.

— By the way ...

Bella drew her legs in beneath her and reached for her cup.

— I met Norman last night and he was very keen to know that you would be here tonight.

— Really.

— Miss Ice. *Really.* Well, yes, he was, *really.* You're such a little fool.

Norman Penrose lived with his father on a thriving estate outside the village of Grange, seven miles distant. In his early thirties, charming and unfailingly courteous in his offers of help in the problems of Longstead, he had always been generous and helpful. And yet, for all his excellent points, Norman made my flesh crawl.

— I'm very sorry, Bella, I said thinly. — I didn't realise that you were so touchy about Norman. Maybe it's you he's really after.

Bella's face assumed a slow, insouciant smile. — I don't think so, darling. My taste in men is somewhat different.

—You mean married.

Bella ran out her tongue and played it on the crown of her upper lip. — Why not?

I felt myself foundering. — What happens if you get caught?

Bella looked at me from drowsy eyes. — London is full of wealthy men with wives in the country. They look after you.

— Please don't get hurt! I blurted, unable to stop myself.

— Don't worry about me, Bella said and stretched like a beautiful, pampered cat. She put her cup and saucer down and looked at me with dreamy curiosity. — May I say something about Norman without having my head bitten off?

— Say it.

— Norman is a catch. There is a war. You are a young girl without experience and, if I may say so, few prospects. Forget your childish feelings for Norman. When you're twenty-five and he's thirty-five, or whatever, it will be very different. Listen to the voice of experience. He admires you greatly.

— And I find him lacking in everything I admire.

— The reality, of course, is that he lacks nothing. He farms nearly two thousand acres. They own half of Belfast.

— Does love mean nothing to you?

Bella's face became spiny. — What do you know about love? Do you think that's all there is in life? Do you think you can eat love and that it can keep you warm? Look at this place! When will you grow up?

Outside, Mr Rafter had materialised and was straining on a rope with Harry.

— I wonder is this the last time? I said.

— Why? asked Bella sharply.

— Mother says we are like a ship without a captain, that Longstead is drifting.

— 'Mother says.' What nonsense! Allan will be Longstead's captain.

— If he comes home.

— How do you mean, 'if'? Of course he'll come home – he has to.

— He's fighting a war, Bella.

— You make life so complicated! she cried. — Certain things are understood. Allan will come home, Longstead will still be here and you will come to realise that the sun rises every morning, with or without love.

I walked through fields that afternoon, down by the lake and over meadows where lambs leapt and tumbled, into woods where our hives were found, through natural pergolas of wild roses and woodbine, and sat on a boulder by a copse from which Longstead could be picked out in the distance. The copse was surrounded by a waist-high wall of large, uneven stones that incorporated a fairy mound where oak trees grew at eccentric angles. The dead had been laid here over millennia, the bodies of warriors brought on handcarts from battle, great chieftains in their cloaks and breastplates and whole clans that had perished in epidemics. No one disturbed a fairy mound lest they troubled the dead, not even my brothers, who used to shoot pigeons here at dusk; they never stood on the mound itself but took up their positions on the perimeter.

Why, as the youngest, I should have to be the worrier, I did not understand. Bella – beautiful, worshipped –

worried only for herself. Lolo, who had married a bishop's son and lived in Fermanagh, would arrive later that day and the whole house would echo to her empty chatter. I was, it seemed, the only person competent to worry. For now, on a day of great peace and confident expectation, as swallows flew high, as men spoke happily about the hay that would be saved, as the whole bounty of the earth seemed to eddy deliciously in the warm air, I sat shivering, my back clammy from a fear I could not name.

Identical twin sisters, the unmarried Misses Carr, who lived a few miles from us and hunted their own pack of harriers, arrived with baskets of home-baked biscuits. They always dressed the same and wore the same shade of lipstick; even their hunters were picked so that no one could tell one from the other. The Misses Carr had a knack of always being in the thick of everything: funerals, christenings, parties. Although my father said they were the most irritating women he had ever met, they were among the few whom Mother counted as her friends.

Daddy's appearance at seven that evening marked the formal opening of proceedings. His stiff, white shirt front and collar seemed an ominous extension of his pallid face. He looked so old. Lifted into his armchair by Harry and placed by the drawing-room fireplace with a glass of champagne, he presided over the embryonic gathering with a lopsided smile.

—You look so dashing, Daddy!

Bella, radiant in a dress of azure voile, her hair piled on her head, her shoulders bare and lovely, bent and kissed him.

—You're good enough to eat, my dear. You both are. My father's strong voice still belied his appearance.

Bella's eyes saw me with amusement. — Our Iz has turned into quite the young woman, hasn't she, Daddy?

— Iz will be here when you'll all have gone, said my father.

— Oh.

— Something wrong, Iz?

—Who's that man? I asked to switch the conversation.

— Him? Bella was unreliable when looking into the middle distance, for her weak eyesight made her peer, a process that robbed her of her beauty. — Oh, he's Ronnie Shaw! He's fun. She dropped her voice. — But they're broke.

The man's profile was sharp and clean and his dark hair swept back from a wide forehead.

— Langley Shaw's son, said Daddy. — His mother is a wonderful woman to have put up with Langley.

— How 'put up with'? I asked.

— Oh, generally, said my father, vague all at once. — He's come up a long way tonight. From Monument.

— He's got a sports car, Bella said. — I'll go and get him.

— Mr Seston!

Norman Penrose was being brought over by Harry. I always went through the same sequence of reactions with Norman: I was at first struck by how tall and handsome he was, immediately followed by a qualification about his eyes, something to do with their ability to be simultaneously intense and void, followed by an endless refining of my first impression until all I was left with was a shell of the original.

—You look so well, sir, Norman said.

Daddy smiled sadly. — How's your father, Norman? Has he got over your poor mother yet? God, but she was a lovely woman. That was a dreadful blow to him to have her taken like that. Would he not come tonight?

— He's in Dublin. Business, I'm afraid.

— I used to like Dublin, you know. Liked lunch in my club. But liked coming home here better.

— A good judge as always, Norman said, and then looked at me with a cautious smile. — Ismay?

— Norman.

— Am I allowed a dance tonight?

— By all means.

— Then that will be the highlight of my evening.

— I'll be keeping a close eye on both of you, Harry said.

— How is Mount Penrose? Daddy asked. — Are you having any trouble from these agitators?

— Well, after a fashion, although I've heard it said that the main thing that agitates them is the lack of porter.

Bella laughed and fanned herself.

— I daresay, but it has to be stopped before it grows out of control, Daddy said.

Norman's lips became two grim lines. — There was a meeting near Grange last week, torches and banners. My father says it's all Mr de Valera.

Daddy shook his head in despair. — Mr de Valera, Mr de Valera. Is there any end to the trouble caused by Mr de Valera?

— At least he's cracking down on the IRA, Norman said.

— Ha! Only after they were allowed to steal the Irish army's entire stock of ammunition! Daddy cried. — Law and order went out the window in this country in 1922. I could have lived anywhere in the world, Australia, the American Midwest, but I came back here. Now I think I made the wrong decision.

— Of course you didn't, Daddy! Bella said.

Daddy leaned forward in his chair. — You know Rafter, our local merchant?

— Little fat chap? Norman said.

— He's not a bad man, all things considered, Daddy said, bound up in his own world. — His son's had himself elected to the local council and Rafter tells me he thinks he can get them to hold the line as far as Longstead is concerned. Ah, the belle of the ball!

Mother looked young in a startling way, just as my father looked old. I recognised the dress as the one last brought out for Lolo's party – emerald silk, its hem to the floor. She gave her cheek to Norman. The twin Misses Carr hovered behind her, but when Daddy glared at them, they took off.

— Norman, you made it, Mother said. — Have you seen Iz?

— How could I have missed her?

— Isn't she lovely?

— Mother!

— Absolutely lovely, Norman said with huge seriousness and Mother went blind with happiness.

Daddy reached to Mother. — Norman's been telling us that these bloody land agitators were over at Grange last week.

— Oh, we mustn't begin the evening with a recitation of our problems, Mother said.

— Ha! I'll be a month dead and you'll wish I was there to recite them for you!

— Let Daddy speak, Mother, said Bella, who always became assertive when Mother appeared.

— All I was attempting to say, said Daddy grimly, was that Rafter has a feel for what's going on at a local level. They could be out there at this moment planning to march on Longstead tonight and we wouldn't know.

— I hope they don't come tonight, we'd scarcely have enough food, said Mother blithely.

Daddy was angry. — It's not a laughing matter! We're not going to give in without a fight!

— One of us should get elected on the council.

A silence gripped the group.

— For God's sake, Iz, Daddy growled, you're not going to end up like that dreadful Gore-Booth woman, are you?

Bella was looking at her hands, shaking her head, as if to say that I could always be relied on to put my foot in it.

Lolo had just come downstairs and heard the conversation.

— You'd have us end up with our throats cut, she said tightly.

— That's Iz, all right, said Bella.

— Iz has a point.

My father closed his eyes in resignation, a reflexive gesture to Mother's voice whenever it entered an argument.

— How are we ever going to have a say in our own country if we don't become involved? Mother asked.

I could see that Norman was amused.

— You have to go out and work to get elected, Mother, said Bella with great patience.

Mother frowned. — What's wrong with that?

I said, — Exactly! There's nothing to stop one of us from

being elected. Then we wouldn't have to rely completely on the likes of Mr Rafter to save our skins.

— Rafter's all right, my father growled.

— I'll vote for you, Iz, said Harry.

— These people are no different to the IRA! Lolo cried. — They'll stop at nothing until England is driven from Ulster!

— Well, I must say I can't blame them, Mother said. — It's high time Ireland was left to govern itself.

— You'll end up behind bars if you don't come to your senses! Daddy shouted.

Bella drew herself up and raised her chin.

— Land agitation is a fad. What fools we would look if we jumped onto councils and things and then the fad ended. We would be far worse off than we are now.

— Hear, hear, said my father and he and Norman raised their glasses.

— What a load of bloody nonsense, Harry said so only I could catch his words.

I wanted to say so much all at once, but Bella's aura and beauty seemed impregnable. I went through the hall and out to the lawn and crossed it to a wall in which a seat was set. The sound of stringed instruments being tuned crept from the dining room. On the gravelled sweep that circled Longstead, cars were parked, their angled hoods and big headlamps silhouetted against the deepening sky.

— Do you smoke?

I jumped. — Oh!

— I saw you come out.

Ronnie Shaw snapped open a metal lighter and flame shot up between us. — We once lived in a place as nice as this.

— What happened?

— The Land Commission took it.

— I'm sorry.

— Gave my father worthless pieces of paper. In one way, it's all quite amusing. I mean, my father was hopeless at managing things, so you could say we're better off. There's no more of this wondering what's going to happen. We sleep soundly. We live our lives.

— Where?

— In a place called Sibrille, it's on the sea near Monument. Do you know Monument?

— I'm afraid not.

— But you've heard of it.

— Of course I've heard of it.

— Everyone has heard of Monument, the same way as they've heard of Venice.

— Come on!

— Monument's built on the loveliest river in the world. It rises from its quays, a town of tiers and terraces. Mediterranean, they say. You can almost smell the olives. You're Iz.

— Yes.

— You're very pretty, he said, looking directly at me. A gap divided his two front teeth.

— What did you call the place you live in?

— I'm serious. The prettiest girl here by a long shot.

— Mr Shaw, do you always go at such a headlong gallop?

— It's Ronnie. We live in the lighthouse in Sibrille. On really stormy days, we can't get out.

— I don't believe you.

— You don't believe anything I say. He crossed his legs and blew smoke into the air. —You must come and see it some day.

— We know very little about the sea here, I said.

— It becomes part of you. Lives in your ears and your nose. Like a woman.

— Whatever that means.

— Means one comes to live for it. Or her. Sailors see the sea as a woman. He flicked his cigarette and it sailed away into the bushes in an arc of red sparks. — You're not horsey.

— How do you know?

— Your sister Lolo told me. She said, 'That's Iz. She hates horses.'

— I don't. She didn't.

— There you go again. She even told me your age.

— My age is none of your business.

— Twenty.

— I'm twenty-one.

— Doesn't matter to me. In fact, it's a novelty to meet someone who's not half horse. My father and mother do nothing else except hunt in the winter, four days a week, and trek around gymkhanas in summer, trying to flog horses to wealthy English people. You'd like the sea, though, I can tell.

— Of course you can't tell, you've barely met me.

— It's not difficult. A pretty girl who prefers the garden on her own to a crowded house. Odds on she'll like the sea.

— I have been to the sea.

— Not one like ours, I bet. Different every day. We have waves as tall as your oak trees.

— You're such a liar.

— Twice as tall sometimes. They break ships the size of your house to matchwood against the rocks. More than a hundred soldiers and seamen drowned off Sibrille after the

Napoleonic wars. There's a tablet to them. Yet for all that, we still call the sea a woman.

— No one owns the sea, I said.

— Why do you say that?

— Here everything is about what you own. Which means land, I suppose. There are more problems owning than not owning, I think. You said as much yourself. You said you sleep soundly.

— Did I?

— 'We live our lives', you said.

— Not only is she pretty, but she forgets nothing.

I ground my cigarette out. — Do you?

Ronnie Shaw was looking directly in through the open windows of the drawing room. — Who's that woman?

I looked. Bella was standing at a window, talking to Norman.

— That's Bella, my sister.

Ronnie's fingers went to the slim case and he took out a fresh cigarette.

— Good Lord, she's gorgeous, he said, almost to himself, and tapped both ends of the cigarette against the polished silver.

I was suddenly weak. Bella's beauty only emphasised how irrelevant I was to a man like this, and how much I still had to learn. Then I felt his hand on my bare arm.

— But not half as gorgeous as you.

— I beg your pardon?

— We never discussed when I will have the pleasure of showing you the lighthouse which you don't believe in, did we?

His engaging smile.

I freed myself. — No, we didn't, Mr Shaw, and we never shall.

I spent the rest of the party, or of much of it as I could, sitting by the range in the kitchen as the staff hurried in and out with plates and trays and teapots. It was the one place I was sure that Norman Penrose would never enter, but each time I reappeared in the marquee, he immediately put down his glass or plate or indeed his current dancing partner and cornered me. The kitchen was my haven. At two in the morning, I went up the back stairs and into bed and slept deeply, dreaming of men in battle and enormous black rooks flocking into night roosts.

— Iz! *Iz!* Wake up!

Bella went to the heavy curtains and pulled them back. Light flooded in whitely.

— Are you awake?

I had gone under the blankets.

— Iz! This is important!

— What time is it?

Bella was dressed and she was smiling at her most engaging. — Nine o'clock. Listen, you and I are going to do something absolutely mad today.

— Go away. I want to sleep.

Bella sat down beside me. — You know Ronnie Shaw? He wants us to go down to Monument.

— He *what?*

— He's playing a rugby match and he wants us to go down and watch it. It's only a few hours in his car. Come on!

I sat up. — He wants you, Bella, not me.

Bella's eyes were intensely bright. — He suggested we both go! Come on! It's something different!

— I don't want to go to Monument with him. He's pompous, I said and went back under the bedclothes.

I felt Bella kneel on the bed and catch the sheet where I was clutching it; she tugged until she fell out on the floor, all my bedclothes around her head. We were both laughing.

— Ronnie's not the worst when you get to know him, she said.

— He thinks you're gorgeous.

— They have no money, but he's fun. I mean, this is just a fun idea.

— Then you go with him.

— You know I won't go on my own. Please, Iz.

— I don't want to go down the country as a sort of chaperone to you, Bella.

— Why not? I'd do it for you.

— No, you wouldn't.

— It's not as if your whole life will end because you spend a day in Monument.

— I don't want to go.

Bella's face darkened and I felt suddenly sorry for her that so much seemed to depend on so little.

— You're a spoilsport, you know that? she said. — You're going to embarrass me.

— Why on earth should I embarrass you?

— Because I thought this was something you'd like to do. That's what I told Ronnie.

— You've actually told him I'm coming, haven't you?

— Oh, for God's sake, Iz! It's not as if I'm asking you to elope! Look, please, as a treat for my birthday, please

151

say you'll come. I've told him we must be back by evening.

In the end, it was not so much that it was easier to let Bella have her way than the fact that I saw her all at once as a woman who was essentially floundering in life, whose beauty and poise should have delivered her so much more than a fast and racy life in which the leaping into a car on a whim and dashing to the other end of Ireland was the pinnacle of achievement.

— What about all the work here? I asked.

— I've seen to everything! she cried. — Thank you, little sister! She ran to the door, then turned back. — Well, come on! He says he has to be down there by two!

As I got dressed, I felt excited, despite myself, that I was embarking on what was, in my life, an adventure. An hour later, having eaten breakfast and said goodbye to my parents, sitting sideways in the tiny rear seat of an MG Midget behind Ronnie Shaw and Bella, we drove down the avenue of Longstead.

— You see? Ronnie said, turning around, a grin cracking his face. — You may get to see the sea much sooner than you imagined.

❧

My chief memory of the journey was of the smoke from Ronnie Shaw's cigarette. Although he pulled in near Carlow and folded down the roof, an ever-floating tail of smoke lay across my face and made me dizzy. Bella and Ronnie chatted the whole time, mostly about people we all knew, people like ourselves who lived in Down and Donegal and County Clare. The social lives of this extended group, their comings and goings to and from London, their war — *their* war! — their marriages and infidelities, their vanities, offspring, disloyalty and appearance were analysed without cease or remorse. Or so I assume, as I went to sleep and, when I came to, found that we were coming in along a busy quay. It was a wider river than I had seen before and its ships and sailing boats were moored right up to the town. Horse-drawn broughams and drays slowed our progress. I smelled ship-bound pens of waiting pigs and cattle before I saw them. Behind me, the brightly painted face of Monument appeared, shop fronts and hall doors, brass knobs and striped, protective door sheets.

We made our way up through the town, Ronnie leaning on the horn to clear the street of children and cyclists. Women in black shawls, their skirt hems to the cobblestones, stood behind carts piled with apples. Most of the shops had awnings rolled out to protect their windows from the sunlight.

— It's hardly Bond Street, but you can buy most things here, Ronnie said and Bella smirked, since the remark had been for her.

We drove up a steep hill and passed through what seemed like tenements; then we were out again in open country with hedgerows on either side and fields of aftergrass. The match, Ronnie explained, was a 'little pipe-opener' that always took place before the season proper got underway, between Monumentals, the local rugby club, and a team from Limerick. Several cars and a great many bicycles were parked in a field in which a tent had been pitched. Beyond the far ditch, I could see the crosses and headstones of a cemetery.

— This is our rugby club, Ronnie said, getting out and reaching to help me.

— It's just a field! Bella cried, as if something far greater had been promised. — And it's beside a graveyard!

— Which is very handy, Ronnie said. — Someone gets done over during a match, we just heel them straight in.

Bella's jaw dropped and Ronnie turned to me and smiled and I saw something deeper in his eyes than I had been expecting.

— Back in a minute, he said and made his way to the tent.

— I don't know about you, Bella said, but I'm starving.

A few other people were waiting around, chatting and giving us shy, sidelong glances. Ronnie emerged less his jacket and with the top of his shirt unbuttoned. He was followed by a big red-headed man in his mid-twenties. The man was limping.

— This is Tom King, Ronnie said and introduced us. He turned to Tom. — The girls have come down from County Meath to see how rugby is really played.

— You must have very little else to do, Tom said, as Ronnie disappeared again.

He had sprained his foot, he explained to us, otherwise he too would have been playing. His face was round and freckled and he spoke in an accent that was gently guttural.

— I beg your pardon, Bella said, but is there by any chance someplace we could find something to eat?

— Not unless you go back into town, Tom said. — Would you like me to see if there are sandwiches inside?

— Thank you so much, Bella said and lifted her chin.

She had a way of being condescending to people who she considered of lesser social standing than us that was beyond her power to correct or alter, an imperious manner she believed was intrinsic to her position but which, when seen at times like this, was simply ridiculous. I could see that she was disappointed, that she had had in mind a glittering occasion, an event such as polo or cricket which followed house parties in England, a social set piece played out in surroundings of wealth and privilege rather than a ramshackle game of rugby in the Irish countryside.

Tom came out carrying a plate of thickly cut sandwiches and a pot of tea. He put plate and pot down on the grass, then went back in for cups and milk.

— I don't believe it – *white* bread, Bella said, her teeth clenched.

— For God's sake, I muttered, don't you ever stop complaining?

— This is turning into a disaster, Bella said.

The wind got up as big, creamy-legged men in shorts appeared. Ronnie emerged looking like an enormous schoolboy. He pranced around as they all warmed up, and threw the oval ball to his team-mates and occasionally leaped into the air. I looked at Bella, shivering and miserable, and it suddenly began to drizzle. Ronnie Shaw had been her whim this morning, and perhaps last night he had chatted her up the same way as he had me. Now, I saw bitterness in her face as she became aware of my amusement, and, for the first time, I realised that of the two of us, I was more beautiful.

The referee blew his whistle and the teams ran at each other. I felt the sudden need to be held by a man, to know more of love than the dear love of my parents. To be possessed. There was a scrum and all that was visible of Ronnie was his backside. Nor was it the coquettish love that Bella spoke of that I yearned for, but love that was deep and lasting. The ball appeared between Ronnie's legs and he heeled it on backwards. The scrum-half seized the ball and, in a graceful movement that made me draw in my breath, became airborne. His fair hair, as he sailed, fluffed out around his head. I smiled for the elegance of him, whoever he was, for the lovely shape of his body in midair, for his extended limbs. Out flew the ball from his hands and he came down softly. Then, there was another scrum and his opposite number put the ball in, but it suddenly shot back out through Ronnie's legs as it had before. I watched again as the scrum-half left the ground in one fluid movement, creating a span of time made entirely of sinew and muscle and spirit, except that, this time, he was facing me. As the ball left his hands and he prepared to meet the ground, he looked directly at me. He smiled.

— Good, isn't he?

Tom was standing beside me. Beyond the ditch at the other side of the pitch, I could see Bella walking among the headstones. It was as if two parts of my brain, hitherto unconnected, had fused, lighting up areas within me that had up to then known only darkness.

— I've never seen someone fly so easily, I said, feeling myself go on fire.

— He's a natural, Tom said. — Goes in under a mountain of men and somehow comes out with the ball.

The scrum-half must have heard him, for there was a ferocious tussle in midfield as enormous men came and threw themselves onto the pile of bodies; and, sure enough, after prolonged cries and screams, a lithe, mud-stained figure with blond hair appeared suddenly from the base of the mêlée and, once again, pitched himself into space. And again, I was sure that our eyes met. This time, I smiled.

— Ronnie told me you live on this enormous estate, Tom was saying. — What's it like?

— Sorry?

My skin was expanding deliciously, as if it was being coaxed out gently in all directions. I wanted to laugh.

— Where you live. What's it like to be brought up somewhere like that? Tom was asking.

— Oh – it's … fine, I stammered. — It's a lovely place.

My happy feeling made my own words seem far off, for I could see only the game being played by one man and heard little. Tom was standing there as if my reply had somehow disappointed him. I had to make an effort. I said,

— None of us has any control over the circumstances into which we're born.

— But we all have a duty to change those circumstances if they are unjust, he said.

I saw the scrum-half again and took a deep, steadying breath. This was fate, I had read. You got up one day and there it was.

— I completely agree, I said.

— I'm glad to hear it, said Tom King.

Out on the pitch, the local team were being pinned back near their own line. I saw Ronnie charging headlong with the ball in his grasp. A huge man flung himself at Ronnie. The impact of their colliding heads sounded like two mallets being struck together. They both went down and the game stopped. I saw a girl run onto the pitch carrying a first-aid kit.

— Jesus, Tom said.

We made our way along the touchline. The man from the visiting team was getting up, but Ronnie was out cold. The girl, her glossy black hair gathered up under a man's peaked cap, knelt beside him. Blood ran from Ronnie's nose. I felt a surge of dismay, for I had begun to realise that there was more to Ronnie Shaw than I had first imagined.

— Ronnie? Ronnie? the girl called.

— Come on now, give him a bit of air everyone, said the fair-haired scrum-half. Then he saw me.

— Hello, I said.

— Hello.

I don't even remember noticing what colour his eyes were, although later I would recall that they were nearer green than blue. Then he turned and went to Ronnie, beneath whose nose the girl was passing a phial. He put his arm around Ronnie's shoulders and sat him up. After a bit, Ronnie's chin came up and then he got to his feet and a blanket was put on his shoulders and he was helped away to loud applause. The crowd dispersed and the game resumed, but I just stood there in the rain, feeling each drop as if they were all made of gold.

— What on *earth* is going on here? asked Bella.

— We thought Ronnie was going into the cemetery, I said, resisting the urge again to shout for my strange happiness.

— I'll be in there shortly if I don't get out of this place, Bella said. — I feel ill.

Over by the ditch, Ronnie sat slumped.

— I'm extremely sorry, he said, looking at me from bulging eyes, but I don't think I'm going to be up to showing you the sea today.

— I'll have to rely on your description, I said. — Are you all right?

— I've never felt better, Ronnie said, and his eyes went glassy and he fell back, his mouth open and the gap between his front teeth pointing for the sky.

Chapter Thirteen

1943

Bella went back to England and Lolo to Fermanagh; Harry had left Longstead while we had been in Monument. With the first day of September came east winds and everyone accepted that the summer was over.

That I had not learned his name made me angry, for I had not had the nerve to ask Tom King when he drove us home in his car, an old bull-nose Morris. And yet, I reasoned as the weeks went by and I heard nothing, had he wanted to know who I was, all he had to do was ask Ronnie. I thought of him most nights and also first thing every morning when I woke to howling winds and the sound of rain dripping from our gutters. I wondered if he ever thought of me. I tried to imagine living in Monument and being able to walk out on Saturdays to the rugby match. I could see him sailing through the air and his green-blue eyes searching the touchline to see if I was there.

&ᷓ◦ᷓ

Daddy's health took a turn for the worse. He must have once been a strong man, for everyone said that his ongoing survival was unprecedented. It was appalling to watch. He went yellow. Light as a child, occasionally he asked for Allan, or made references to jobs to be done about the place, or asked questions about the price of cattle. As the doctor's visits became part of our days, Mr Rafter also began to appear, usually in the late afternoon. A bond had formed between Daddy and Rafter, and now, as the breaking of that bond approached, the grocer came up and calmly dealt with Daddy's ever more rambling questions.

At some stage in this inexorable decline, I became aware that outside the walls of Longstead, local politics were moving steadily against us. 'Agitation' was the recurring word. It floated out from the meetings between Daddy and Mr Rafter. The people outside who were agitating for land they had always been denied were looking in over our crumbling walls and seeing our untilled and untended acres. Daddy's ill health alone was preventing what only a short time ago would have been unthinkable: the surrender of Longstead. And then, one night, when the house was locked and asleep, there came a mighty explosion. I felt terror, as if something that had always lain hidden was now enlarged. The absence of a man was piercing as I made my way downstairs. Wind blew through the shattered window of the drawing room, making the curtains billow. I felt as if we had all been violated. The next morning, one of the farm hands came in and fearfully reported that someone had painted a message on the wall by our gates. I went down with him to see. The bold letters seemed to have been scrawled with venom: *LANDLORDS OUT!*

It seemed futile to say that we were not landlords, that we rented land to no one.

❦

An envelope came addressed to Bella and me: *The Misses Bella and Ismay Seston.* In it was a postcard from Ronnie Shaw or, to be precise, a note scrawled by him on a postcard of his father's: *LANGLEY SHAW MFH, SIBRILLE.* Ronnie had managed to enlist in a regiment of the British army in Northern Ireland, it seemed, and was throwing a party in Monument before he left. A hotel had been booked and bedrooms reserved for us. Ronnie seemed to have recovered.

I sat down and wrote a polite refusal, explaining that Bella was in London and that owing to family commitments, I could not accept. Leaving home, even for a night, when my father lay dying and when rocks were being hurled through our windows was out of the question. I sealed the envelope and put it on the hall table for posting in the village later that day. But then an hour went by and I was helping to prepare my father's lunch when a sudden image transfixed me. It was that of a lithe body suspended in the air. I went out to the hall and sat, trying to come to terms with what I felt. A weakness, even a helplessness. I could not bring myself to call it a craving, but I had to see him again, even if it meant abrogating all the many responsibilities that I had taken on. Feeling reckless and dizzy, I tore up the first letter and wrote another, explaining that Bella was in London, but saying that I would love to come.

❧

Mr Rafter's son, the one on the council, had a van with an anthracite roof burner: he drove me across the border of Meath into County Kildare on a Friday morning. I had left written instructions as to Daddy's regime and had made everyone recite back to me what was to happen at the key times: when he needed changing and turning and how his hot water bottle was to be kept hot and wrapped in a towel and what pills he had to take and when. Mother kissed me goodbye without a care in the world, which almost made me change my mind; but by then John Rafter's van was waiting at the hall door.

—What's going to happen? I asked, as we drove between fields of cattle.

John Rafter was an almost comical reproduction of his father, and although he was not as neat or natty and always seemed in need of a shave, he had shaken off the obsequiousness that was part of Mr Rafter.

— It's a faction, Iz, just a faction, he said.

I asked what he meant.

— People will go to extremes in times of hardship, and there's a lot of hardship around at the minute. It's just unfortunate that – you'll forgive me – that there's no able-bodied man in Longstead.

— My brother is fighting a war.

— There's a faction out there that pays no heed to that at all. Forgive the language, but with only two women in your place, the bastards have nothing to fear or lose.

— Are we alone in being attacked like this?

— Not at all, it's happening all over, John Rafter said, as if reassurance lay in widespread intimidation.

— Where? I haven't heard. Are the Penroses waking up to messages painted on their property? Are they getting rocks hurled through their windows?

John looked over at me kindly. — That's a different set-up, Iz. In that case, the faction would have too much to lose.

— I don't understand.

— There's twenty men employed by the Penroses. Add in their families and you have a hundred people depending on a weekly wage. They have out-farms thirty miles from Grange. They have £100 given to heat the school. At Christmas, every Penrose cottage got a goose, a ham and six bottles of porter. Those people are much better off with the Penroses there than with trying to put them out.

We had arrived at a tiny railway station and for the second time that morning, I felt an overpowering urge to stay at home, but John was smiling at me.

— You go on now and stop worrying. I'll be here at twelve tomorrow to collect you.

— Thank you, I said and to my own great surprise, and I'm sure to his too, I leaned over and kissed his grainy cheek.

Within half an hour, I had forgotten Longstead. The train plunged through tawny fields and cooling stands of trees from which spouts of slate-grey pigeon erupted, by way of luminous lakes, by somnolent villages where ass-carts stood with their load of a single milk churn and youths with hurling sticks paused to wave. We crossed rivers with cattle on their banks and paddocks of sleek, indignant horses, and went by cottages with sleeping black cats on their steps and pigs out the back. I marvelled that the train could take in so much in its journey, that Ireland was not just one country but a collection of so many different places. I saw mountains whose flanks were covered in stands of timber and in whose high pleats the ivory-like flecks of cattle were imbedded. Across the carriage corridor, the masts of ships came into view.

At the station, a jarvey took my bag and I boarded a horse-coach that surely hadn't seen daylight for over a century but which now, with the Emergency, had been brought back into service. As we set out down the quayside, the hooves of the big Irish draught sang on the cobblestones. The tidal river, the power in its midstream, the way the large ships looked at its mercy, and the trawlers, all slapping up and down to the river's command, excited me unaccountably. I had, I knew, spent every minute since I had left here waiting to come back.

—The Commercial Hotel, Miss, said the jarvey, opening the hatch.

I looked up and saw how the whole town seemed to be in a pile, houses where one expected sky, and seagulls perched on the utmost chimney pots.

The hall of the hotel, floored in terracotta tiles, was dim. I went to a desk for my key and heard, from an inner bar, the swelling sound of drinking men. Ronnie had written to say that he would call in at three and take me out to see the sea at Sibrille. My bedroom overlooked the river and I sat for an hour, absorbing the contrast with what I was used to, the port activity and throngs of people in place of stillness; but after waiting another half an hour for Ronnie, I went out to explore.

Never was there a moment that day that I did not love Monument. I was not to know then, of course, how it might be in rain or storms or, once every ten years or so, in snow, but, that day, sunlight infused every façade and pediment, every alleyway and wrought-iron gate, each set of steps disappearing, it seemed, between tight buttresses or facing gables on their way to the clouds. I had not been prepared for the size of the town, since the bulk of it lay concealed in successive terraces, behind old battlements, through gates that revealed tiny courtyards, in unsuspected squares from which the river could be made out far below one's feet. Where did he live, I wondered? What did he do? And if he looked out of his window and saw me, would he remember that we had met, however briefly, once before?

It was not Ronnie's party at all but the annual supper dance of the Monumentals rugby club. The banner of the club, white with tassels at both ends and the letters MONUMENTALS either side of a crouching lion, the club's emblem, was slung high across the hotel's dining room. On a raised platform at one end, four elderly men in dinner jackets were playing musical instruments. The room was crowded and already too warm.

—You'll like us down here, Ronnie said with his roguish smile as he held the tips of my fingers and then brought them to his lips. — We're a mixed lot, not nearly as grand as the crowd you knock around with.

— I already do like you down here, I said.

The band started up another tune and Ronnie led me out onto the little dance floor.

— I'm sorry too about not turning up earlier, he said, but the car broke down.

— It doesn't matter, I enjoyed my afternoon.

— I would have liked to have shown you the sea. People who haven't seen it before gasp.

— I have, as I have told you more than once, seen the sea.

— But not this one, as I have told you.

I laughed. The band, stumbling through some of its faster routines, reminded me of an old spluttering car, yet Ronnie danced well and we glided around.

—You shine, you know, Ronnie said.

— It's hot in here.

—You are radiant, is what I mean.

—When are you off?

— I'm serious.

— There you go, headlong again. Tell me when you're off.

— First thing tomorrow morning.

— Oh. I hadn't realised.

— Happened all of a sudden. I go to barracks in Belfast tomorrow and enlist. With luck, I'll be shipping within a month.

— My brother is with the Royal Engineers. I wish he weren't.

—Why so?

—There's no one at home to run the place. We may lose it to the Land Commission.

— Join the club, Ronnie said.

We swept by our table where a thin beef broth had already been served.

— May I tell you something? Something important? Ronnie asked.

— By all means.

—When I got your letter, I jumped three feet in the air.

—You should be more careful.

— I couldn't care tuppence if I'd broken my neck. Your being here has made this evening for me. I'm on the moon.

— I think they're serving the main course, I said.

We ate boiled bacon and cabbage and drank glasses of brown ale. The people at the table, to whom I had been introduced but whose names I could not remember, chatted about rations and the war and what lay before Ronnie. Some of them asked me polite questions about Dublin, which they had been to once or twice, but mostly they were happy in their familiarity with one another, laughing about incidents from rugby matches and feats of daring of which I had no knowledge.

I had been searching for him since I had come in, hoping that it would not be obvious, but ultimately not caring if it was. He was nowhere to be seen. Neither was Tom King, the man who had driven us home. Perhaps they didn't live in Monument. Perhaps they had left and gone to live elsewhere, in England, for example, where good jobs were to be had in war industries. Ships sailed from Monument to Wales every other day.

Rice with custard was served. Ronnie kept getting up and dancing with women from other tables. Then I looked up and saw him. He had just come in and was standing at the door with Tom King. The girl I had seen on the rugby field, her glossy dark hair now at her shoulders, was beside him.

Ronnie went over to the door and had his back slapped. He kissed the girl's cheek. She was tall, with strong, striking features. Her arm was linked through that of the man whose image I had woken to every day for weeks. Ronnie was laughing and saying, — She's right over here.

I wanted to run. I had made a huge mistake.

— This is Iz, the most beautiful woman in County Meath, Ronnie boomed. — Tom you already know. May I introduce you to Frank and Alice Waters?

We shook hands. The girl looked me over, slowly, up and down. I wanted to die. I could scarcely bring myself to look at him. Ronnie had seized Alice and made for the dance floor.

— This is the lady I drove all the way to the County Meath, Tom was saying.

— I know, Frank said.

— Would you like a drink, Iz? Tom asked.

— No, thank you.

Tom made his way towards the bar and Frank sat in Ronnie's chair. I saw everything blurred. Where before there had been light inside me, now there was dimness and dismay. It had never occurred to me that he might be married. He said, — We've met before.

— Have we? I don't remember.

— You were down for our pipe-opener. When Ronnie got knocked out.

— Oh, that. I'd forgotten about that.

He smiled. — I haven't. Ronnie talks about you non-stop.

— Non-stop? I don't think so.

— I'm not surprised.

— What does he say, then?

— That you're the youngest of several sisters, that you

live on one of these enormous estates. That you live a charmed life.

— Ronnie knows very little of my life, I said dismissively. — And our estate is by no means enormous.

— The fact that you live on any kind of an estate is important for Ronnie because the Shaws never stop talking about the enormous estate they used to own. But they lost it.

— Do you approve of that?

— Oh, no, I think it's tragic, he said and the side of his mouth played with a little smile.

He was trying to make me rise, which wasn't difficult, because I was seething at myself for the assumptions I had made and the long journey I had undertaken for nothing.

— I'm sure it was tragic for the Shaws, I said tightly.

— Not half as tragic as it was for the hundreds of tenants who had been grubbing a living from Shaws for centuries, he said.

From the corner of my eye, I saw his beautiful wife gliding around the floor with Ronnie and I felt profoundly foolish.

— Every case is different, I said. — We, for example, have no tenants and yet we live in fear of our lives from people who throw rocks through our windows under cover of darkness.

He blew his cheeks out. — There's no excuse for that, but look at it their way. I bet you live behind walls. These people have lived for hundreds of years outside those walls. But now, suddenly, it's dawned on them that they run this country, they make the laws. And the people inside the walls, except for their land, have no power any more. They have no allies and, with respect, no meaning. What's happening is inevitable.

On any normal day, I would have agreed with him wholeheartedly, but I hated myself so much at that moment that I wanted him too to despise me.

— Are you some kind of politician, Mr Waters? I asked.

I could see how clear his eyes were and how deeply one could delve into them.

— No, just someone who cares about their country.

— It will all lead to ruin, I said, hearing Bella in my voice. — If you can't distinguish between patriotism and theft, then I feel very sorry for you.

I was irking him, yet he struggled to keep his composure.

— You're angry. Why?

— I'm not angry, I replied, furious with myself. — I just hate the politics of people who ignore the feelings and circumstances of others. What about law? What about fairness?

— Where's the fairness in the fact that ninety-five per cent of the wealth of this country is owned by three per cent of the people? he asked and his cheeks all of a sudden blazed.

— If I may say so, I said, that's a half-baked philosophy that allows people who own nothing to take what isn't theirs.

I was blazing too, but I didn't care. I wanted to burn any question or hint of affection that might have existed, however ephemerally, between us. I wanted never to be in this place again. I wanted to go home.

— I'm sorry if I've upset you, he said, getting up. — I hope you enjoy your time here.

I went out to the ladies room and stayed there for twenty minutes. I had been prepared to come and risk Ronnie's

advances in the hope of meeting the man I had dreamed of;
and now that I had met Frank Waters, and Alice, his wife,
all I could wish for was that the time until the train left the
next morning might somehow dissolve and that I could
leave Monument. I was trembling with frustration. If I had
taken the merest precaution of asking a simple question
during the five hours it had taken Tom to drive us home
the last time, I could have prevented this disaster. I think I
had been afraid of Bella, who had commandeered the front
of the car, afraid of her picking up my interest and her
subsequent reaction, which would have been one of scorn.
But it was no use blaming Bella. The thought that Frank
might have sensed my interest and was amused by it added
further vinegar to the wound. I put my head into my hands
and shrieked into my lap for my embarrassment.

I emerged some time later, resolved: I would tell Ronnie
I was ill and that I would have to retire early. As I made my
way towards the dining room, I heard shouts. The band had
stopped. A commotion was ensuing near the door and I
realised that the rugby club's banner had been torn down.
A woman screamed. I heard a shout of *Up the Republic!* Half
a dozen men or more were struggling to regain possession
of their banner from a diminutive bearded figure who had
been wrestled to the floor. A man to the left of the ruck led
with his foot. The circle around the fallen man closed.

— Kill the little fucker!

— Dirty Shinner!

The sight was appalling, a man on the ground being
kicked.

— *Get away from him!* Alice Waters flew at the kicking
men like an enraged hawk. — *Stop it!* she screamed

She clawed at them, trying to drag them off, but they

172

scarcely noticed. Blood appeared on the fallen man's face, or what I could see of it. Some of his attackers fell over in their eagerness. Then, in a movement so fast that it was hard to follow, Frank Waters was in the thick of it, diving to the floor. It might have been a rugby match. Seconds later, he was in the centre of the crowd, a space cleared around him, panting, standing over the fallen man.

— That's enough!

— Fucking little republican bastard! swore one man. He drew back his foot again. Frank punched him square between the eyes and he went down.

— I said, that's enough! Frank shouted and faced them. — No one's getting killed here unless I do it! Now get back! And you, get up, Stephen Duggan, and hand over our flag!

Slowly, the man got up, blood on his mouth and in his beard. His eyes were crazy.

— God help you all that you have to play a British game in Monument, he said thickly, still clutching the banner.

There was a threatening, collective roar. Frank snatched the flag from the man's hands and threw it into the centre of the room. He put his arm around the man's shoulders.

— Let's go home, he said.

Although Tom King made a presentation of cuff links in the shape of rugby balls to Ronnie, and Ronnie spoke of his chances of coming home from war in one piece being much greater than surviving a training session with Monumentals, a remark which everyone cheered, the mood was sombre, as if a basic fissure had opened and ugliness had been revealed. I saw Tom come in with Alice's coat and then go out with her. Ronnie was being brought drinks at the bar, but I had declined all offers of alcohol and said that I was going to bed.

— We're not like you think we are.

Tom had come back in and was sitting beside me.

— I'm not shocked, really. These things happen, I said.

— It was bad form, he said. — It ruined the evening.

— Who is he? I asked.

— Stephen Duggan. His father's a blacksmith, they live in Balaklava. They're decent people.

— And is Stephen decent?

— He's too hot, but at least he's got courage.

— To pull down a banner at a dance?

— He's got opinions, Tom said quietly. — It's dangerous at the moment to have opinions in Ireland. There's emergency legislation, I'm sure you're aware of it. The Special Branch shoot people like Stephen with republican sympathies. Men are dying in jail on hunger strike. Men are hanging for their beliefs.

— He seemed to go home when Mr Frank Waters told him to, I observed dryly. — I expect he's a republican too.

— Frank and his sister grew up beside the Duggans, Tom said. — They're childhood friends.

I felt my mouth go dry.

— Frank and his sister?

— Frank and Alice, yes. Tom looked at me. — Are you all right?

I sat at the window of my bedroom, looking out over the night wharves, all but invisible because no lights were permitted because of the war, and at the occasional vessel slinking into port or downstream through the black folds of the river.

I had never felt so miserable. The thought of what I had done, of how deliberately rude I had been to him, of how successfully I had ruined what I had set out to accomplish, drove me so deep that I was ill. The day that had begun with such brightness and hope now lay irretrievably broken. I imagined him lying on a bed in his house somewhere in the town above me, his fair hair on the pillows, and the thought made my blood plunge. A knock came to the door.

— Who is it?

— May I come in? asked Ronnie.

I sat on the bed, my feet beneath me, and he sat in the only chair. He looked sterner and somewhat older, perhaps to do with the light, or as if the imminent prospect of enlisting had seasoned him all of a sudden.

— I thought I'd say goodbye, he said.

— We've said goodbye, Ronnie.

— We said goodnight, he said and lit a cigarette. — You don't mind me being up here?

— Why should I mind?

— A girl on her own away from home and so on.

— I'm quite independent, don't worry.

— That's one of the many thing I like about you.

— And I'm very tired.

— May I say one thing? He had a way of smiling that was halfway between roguish and the embodiment of integrity. — May I ask you a question that I sincerely hope you have not been asked before?

— Which question?

— Iz, will you marry me?

I gaped at him. He had actually gone down on his knees. I began to laugh. — Is this some sort of prank?

He looked up at me mournfully.

— From the very moment I first saw you in the garden of your home, I wanted you. I cannot get you out of my mind. You have taken root in my imagination. I know this all sounds absurd, but I cannot go away tomorrow to join an army and fight a war without knowing that you will be here for me when I come back.

— Ronnie, I said, I've met you twice before. I like you and think you are a fine, brave man, but that is all. Please get up.

— May I write to you then? he asked, remaining on his knees. — Please give me something. I'm dying for you. I'm sick of the thought of life without you.

He looked so abject that I had to bite my lip to stop myself laughing outright.

— Write by all means, but please don't expect me to reply. I know you're going off in the morning and I wish you the very best, but it would be foolish to think that something might await us when you return. We'll always be friends, of course.

— Is there someone else?

I felt my blood plunge again and suck with it my womanhood.

— No. There is no one else.

— Excellent! Ronnie, beaming, was on his feet. — May I then ask one favour? That you write and tell me if there is someone else? That way, I'll know not to go on hoping.

— Ronnie, I don't see why I should agree to do that.

— At least give me the luxury of self-delusion.

I stood up. — I will write to you, but like a sister. And

now I think it's time you went home. You've got an early start.

He kissed my cheek. — Please remember, I do love you and always will, he said.

CHAPTER FOURTEEN

1943–44

It would be a sombre winter in Longstead. And, yet, when Daddy rallied and sat up in bed, asking for bean soup, Mrs Rainbow spoke of the power of prayer and doubled her rosaries.

I woke on the first morning of December to a white world. Although the house was piercingly cold, it was worth it just to be able to behold our trees etched in perfection, our normally lumpy paddocks made smooth.

I trudged out through our temporarily forgiven acres and walked until my legs ached. In the intense silence, looking back on the house, one could imagine that this was not home to a dying man and his penniless family, but rather a magic kingdom full of life and plenty.

In the three months since the dance in Monument, I had received half a dozen letters from Ronnie Shaw: two posted from Belfast and the rest from somewhere in Scotland. I could not but smile as he described fox hunting in the border country, as if fox hunting was what war preparation was all about. I wrote back, for I admired his persistence and, to be honest, felt touched by the fact that he admired me. But that was all. My letters were brief and I took care over them so that Ronnie could not draw any inferences about my feelings. I liked him, I conceded; he was a likeable man. But liking him was an ocean away from what I sought.

During the weeks following the dance, I had cursed myself every day for my own stupidity. I could see no way back. Frank Waters would see me as an arrogant member of a class that he despised – and he would be entirely justified. I thought about writing to apologise, but it would have been fruitless, because there was no way I could explain how jealousy and disappointment had given rise to my behaviour. I had successfully accomplished what I had set out to do in the heat of my anger – I had demolished any possibility of a relationship between us.

And then, as winter wore on, I felt the weight of my indiscretion lift from me, little by little. I thought of him less. It could not have worked anyway, I told myself; the gaps were too large. Bella was right after all – I was young and I had no experience. Or at least, I now had one experience, however unsatisfactory and incomplete, and I should learn from it.

Christmas came and went and we burned fires night and day to keep warm. A sense of suspension gripped Longstead, as if everything would remain as it were, however imperfect, for as long as snow lay on the ground. The thaw came with the new year. Leaks abounded. Then in the small hours of one January night, I woke with shouting in my ears. I had been dreaming of Bella and myself, walking together in a city. It was she, I first thought, who was shouting. — *Iz! Iz! Oh, God, Iz, where are you? IZ!*

Then I realised it was Mother.

ॐ≼

Daddy had been so long near death that we had all come to believe the situation could continue indefinitely. He had passed away during the night and by the time we drew back the drapes, he no longer looked like anyone I had ever known.

Lolo and her husband arrived from Fermanagh the next day and the morning after that, from London, Bella and Harry, who had just become engaged to be married to a woman he had met from Somerset. The great excitement was that Allan, on leave in England, was on the mail boat. The kitchen hummed. Rooms we seldom used were opened, fires set and great quantities of ash drawn in to feed them.

I had forgotten what an impression Allan made: he was big and broad, with blond hair and ink-black eyebrows. His eyes were a deep brown. I knew him very little, I realised, since one or the other of us had mostly been away. Of course, I had grown up hearing of his horsemanship and the dedication he had applied to salmon rivers and how he had single-handedly managed Longstead; but now, in the flesh, he looked older than I had imagined. He immediately took on responsibility for all aspects of the funeral, which was just as well, since

Mother was more anxious about the looming social obligations than about the event itself. She sat there in formal clothes, clasping and unclasping her hands, and I knew that but for propriety she would be down the fields, painting.

Mr Rafter came up after supper and spent a long time in discussion with Allan.

— What did he have to say? I enquired later.

— Is he owed money? Bella asked.

— Mr Rafter is our friend, Allan said. — He's on our side.

— So he should be, all the money he's made from us over the years, Bella said.

Her clothes were newly bought and wildly sophisticated to our eyes. She had told Mother the night before that she had met someone in England who she hoped to bring home and introduce. *Sounds like he's got money*, Mother had whispered to me.

— Listen, I don't want to hear you say that again, said Allan sternly. He had become used to command. — Mr Rafter is fighting a rearguard action on our behalf. We'll be lucky to be left with this roof over our heads, the way things are going. All that's been stopping them up to now has been the fact that Daddy was ill.

— They think they can just come in and take what they want, Bella said, but we're going to stop them. She looked to Harry. — What are you smiling about? Why don't you come home and get involved?

— I don't even know how to drive a tractor, Harry said.

— Isn't there some legal way we can approach this problem? asked Bella.

— I'm not sure there is, Allan said. — Thousands of

landless men are banging on the doors of this new Land Commission, demanding acres. A place like ours where proper farming hasn't taken place in twenty years is a ripe prospect.

— But we have to be given a chance! I cried. — *You* have to be given a chance!

— That's exactly it, and Rafter agrees, Allan said. — Once this wretched war is over, I can come back and knuckle down – but that won't happen tomorrow. However, Rafter thinks his son can persuade the Land Commission to hold off.

— I'm sure it suits him to do so, Bella said with scorn, so that he can go on charging us the earth for everything.

— So bloody what if it does suit him? asked Allan darkly, and strode out.

We put Daddy's lead-lined coffin into the vault at Longstead on a day that was warm and bright. When we all returned to the house, it was as if a huge burden had been lifted. In some ways, it was like Bella's party of the summer before – the Misses Carr arrived with baking and went about together, their hands full of plates; Norman Penrose appeared, this time with his father, whose face sprouted curling whiskers and whose expression was ever midway between contemplation and regret.

Mother sat in a corner like a lost child, the Misses Carr either side of her, one of them stroking her hand. Most of the people who were drinking tea and chattering loudly were locals, men like Mr Rafter and farmers from round about and a few corn merchants from Dublin. I wondered was this what a long and once bright life had amounted to? Years of decline and then the day you were coffined and shelved away, all but forgotten within a few of hours?

— Iz, I need you to hear something.

Bella had arrived inside the door of the drawing room, linking Allan in one arm and Norman Penrose in the other. — Norman has just made the most wonderful suggestion. Tell Iz, Norman.

— It's very little, Norman said.

— It certainly is not, Bella said. She drew herself up. — Norman has come to the rescue. He's going to send men over to plough and till and generally fix things up here, aren't you, Norman?

— Only if you so wish, Norman said and looked directly at me.

— That's … very kind, Norman, I said.

— Activity will make it far more difficult for the agitators, Bella said. — Apparently, Norman has offered on umpteen occasions, but Daddy always refused.

What to Bella seemed the ideal solution, to me seemed undue haste. She beamed as she said, — They'll see that Mount Penrose is *involved*.

— Of course, we'll pay you whatever it costs, Allan said.

Norman made brushing motions in the air. — Wouldn't hear of it.

— We can't allow you to do this for nothing, Allan said.

— It's not as if this is just an ordinary commercial trans-action, Norman said and looked at me again.

Bella let go of Allan and linking me with her free arm, drew Norman and me tight to her. — Some things are just understood, isn't that right, Norman?

We were all three in this ridiculous little knot of Bella's

making. Then, as one, we all turned to the door. My mouth dropped open, I knew, but I could do nothing about it.

— Hello, he said.

He said, — Sorry I'm late, but the hackney ran out of fuel five miles down the road and I had to walk.

I had detached myself from Bella and Norman and we were standing in the hall. I could scarcely speak.

— What … what are you doing here?

— Ronnie telegrammed when he heard the news and asked me to represent him. He wants you to know how very sorry he is. And I am too.

I was dizzy. I knew that Bella and Norman were staring at us. I said,

— I need some air. Come on.

We walked down the front avenue and came to the stile into the lake field, so called because in winter water took up most of it. All the feelings for him that I thought I had forgotten returned, not only as if they had never gone away, but with renewed force.

— It's very kind of you to have made such a long trip.

— Ronnie's a good friend, Frank said.

— He writes to me.

— I know. He writes to me too and tells me.

— Tells you what?

— Everything. He says he's going to marry you.

— I don't believe he told you that!

— Is it true?

— Of course it's not true.

Frank smiled. — Ronnie's impulsive. He's like his father, not really connected to the world. Maybe the army will sort him out.

I looked back to the house and could see that the French windows had been opened and that people were drinking their cups of tea on the lawn. Frank took out cigarettes.

— This is a tough day for you, he said quietly.

It was until you arrived, I wanted to say, but instead I blew smoke from the side of my mouth and asked him, — How is your wild friend who tore down the banner that night?

— Stephen? What did you think of him?

— I was frightened. He was so … intense.

Frank's eyes sought out something in the distance. — Stephen believes that the Brits should be put out of the Six Counties. He thinks Ireland should take advantage of the war and strike hard while England's attention is elsewhere.

— Isn't that dangerous talk?

— It's insane. But the funny thing is that just over twenty years ago, it was the talk of heroes.

— For some, I said, despite myself.

— Always, for some, he said.

I thought of the land on which we were standing and the danger posed to it by people like Stephen and maybe even by Frank Waters. So much I didn't know – of life, of my country, of love.

— Why did you save him? I asked.

— Because he's my friend, Frank answered and looked at me. — Just as Ronnie is my friend. You do hard things for your friends.

I realised with a jolt that he had travelled over a hundred miles and walked the last five to present Ronnie's condolences to people who represented everything he despised. I said,

— I'm sorry if coming here has been so hard for you.

He shook his head. — There's something about you, he said.

— I beg your pardon?

— This is not you, he said. — I don't know how I know this, but somehow I do. The girl I saw at the rugby match and the one I met at the dance were completely different. Which one is you?

I wanted to explain so much to him, to tell him that he was right and that it was I who had allowed my own stupidity to sink us before we had ever set sail. But then I saw Bella.

— I think we should go back in now, I said.

Bella stood just inside the hall door, peering out, trying to make out who I was with. Her face clouded as we approached.

— This is my sister. Bella, this is Frank Waters, a friend of Ronnie's, I said as breezily as I could. — He's come up all the way from Monument to be here today.

As they shook hands, I could see Bella's eyes become enlarged with curiosity.

— Ah, the Shaws, she said. — Do you see much of them?

At that moment, Lolo appeared behind Bella and made frantic jerking motions with her head. I went in.

— The Penroses are leaving! Lolo whispered. — Mr Penrose asked to see you.

I walked through the house and out to the stables, where Mr Penrose and Norman were standing by their chauffeur-driven car, the father looking impatiently at his watch, the son smiling as if the very sight of me always led to his enchantment.

— My dear, said Stanley Penrose, placing his hands on my shoulders and composing his face in an expression approaching happiness. — I have admired you since you were a baby. I know you as if you were my own. Before I leave now, I just want to say that from this sad day on, whatever we have is yours. All of it. Want for nothing. Your days of wanting are over.

And so saying, as Norman fixed me with a look of utter knowing, they swept out.

I went upstairs and lay on my bed and shivered. Conversation bubbled from the rooms below. Everything and everyone seemed to be conspiring in my future, their own needs uppermost and mine of no consequence. I was being steered away from my own feelings, just as now, lying on my bed at a moment when the man I wanted most was downstairs, wondering if I might reappear.

I lay there for a good while, then I heard cars starting and footsteps on the gravel. I sat up and looked out the window. He was getting into someone's car. My heart raced so much that I almost couldn't hear. I had one chance and I was going to take it.

— Iz? I had raced down the stairs and passed Bella in the hall. She caught me. — Where on *earth* did *he* come from? she hissed.

—You were introduced to him.

— He's a *dock worker,* she said incredulously.

— Let go of me!

I ran out. The car was nosing away. It belonged to some of Daddy's corn merchant friends and they were giving him a lift.

— Frank!

The car stopped and he climbed out of the back.

— I tried to find you to say goodbye, he said.

— I wanted to write to you after the dance and apologise for my behaviour, but I didn't know what to say, I blurted.

He stared at me. I said,

— The real me was the me at the rugby match.

— I know.

—You do?

—Yes.

— I'm sorry. I was unforgivably rude.

— You were so angry, he said. — I just couldn't make out why.

I closed my eyes. — I thought you were married to Alice. It was myself I was angry at.

I expected him to laugh, but he said nothing for a moment. — Ah.

—You must think I'm a fool.

— Do I look as if I think you're a fool?

My breath was coming fast. — The only reason I came down to the dance was to see you.

His eyes searched my face. The driver of the car was honking on the horn.

— Do you think it might work? Us? he asked.

—Yes, I think it might.

— I'm willing to try it if you are, he smiled.

—Yes, I'm willing to try, I said.

He climbed back into the car and drove away. I said,

— I love you.

CHAPTER FIFTEEN

1944

Except for Allan, everyone left the day after the funeral and the house found a new routine. Spring cleaning began. When Daddy had been alive, he had been the focus of everyone's energy; now jobs that had been put off for years were suddenly commissioned. Mother, of course, took no part, for although being married for years to an invalid was a strain from which she was happy to be released, I knew that part of her had gone with him and that grief respects no logic nor is any less no matter how long awaited.

My joyful mood, inappropriate though it was in the circumstances, carried me like a cork on a flood. Every time I thought of Frank, which was all the time, I smiled, for I was revolving through a galaxy of delight. My happiness was infectious: the girls in the house who were dusting and sweeping were happy too, and sang, as I did, as they brought ancient rugs into the garden and beat out decades of dust. Even as I sang, I knew that nothing but obstacles lay ahead of us, for the obligations in which our family had been reared were clear and, guided above all by the need to retain property, made a grave crime of marrying outside.

I found Allan sitting on the wall of the fairy mound. He held a match to my cigarette, then lit his own.

— When are you going back? I asked.

— Tomorrow.

— Do you like it? I mean, the army?

Allan looked away. — I'd never have joined up except for Daddy.

— Really? I thought you couldn't wait.

— You were away at school. I was trying to get this place back on its feet, but every night he'd start on at me about Ireland's neutrality and about how I was shirking my duty. *My* duty, you know. When I told him the war wasn't Ireland's, he went purple. I eventually joined up just to get away from him.

Allan, I realised, had become idealised in my mind over the years, a distant and absent hero on whom everyone could depend.

— I'm sorry. I didn't know, I said.

— It's the past, it's over now.

— What will you do, now that he's no longer here?

— I have to see it through. I'm an officer, I have obligations to my men. But when it's over, I'll come back here and have Longstead humming within a year. He smiled. — What will you do, Iz?

— Me?

— With your life.

— I hate these kinds of questions.

— But you have dreams.

I watched crows circling, eyeing their nests. — I would like to get away when the war is over. To see a lot more of the world than Longstead.

— And then? To come home?

I looked at him. — I don't think so. It's different for a woman.

He said nothing for a moment.

— I like him, Iz, he said softly.

I stared at my brother, then laughed. — How do you know anything?

— I saw you with him just before he left. The way you were looking at one another. And in the last few days here you've been floating on air.

— Yes, I am happy, I said, still laughing. — But you don't know him.

— I know men, Iz. He and I chatted for nearly twenty minutes the other day. He's a good lad. A bit hot, maybe, but his heart is in the right place. He'll go far.

— What did you talk about?

— The war. Like everyone, he wants to know when it will end. About Ireland. Ronnie Shaw. Allan grinned. — He told me that Ronnie wrote and said he's been beagling in Scotland.

Wind swept through the top branches of the bare trees above us.

— Bella will have a fit, I said.

— Forget Bella, Allan said. — Forget this place and all the nonsense. Follow your heart.

— Do you really mean that?

— Of course I do. We've only got one life. You've got to live your dreams. No one else is going to do that for you.

— It won't be easy.

— I know, but he's worth it. I know that, Alan said. — And so do you.

❧

True to his word, Norman Penrose began to show up with men and with horses harnessed to ploughs. Paddocks were turned and fencing was seen to in fields which in spring would graze cattle. Norman could often be seen walking our land with his foreman, pointing to this and that with the blackthorn stick he always carried. Afterwards, he invariably called in and was given tea, but I kept a good eye out and managed to avoid many of these visits.

Frank had written to me as soon as he got back to Monument. His letters matched my mood – they over-flowed. I wrote back to him and asked him to come up again as soon as he could. I thought of nothing else except about how he would suddenly appear, as he had the last time, and of all the things we would then have to say and do together.

A letter came from Ronnie in February. It was written with a tone of resignation. It seems that he and Allan had met somewhere in the south of England. I could just imagine poor Ronnie bubbling away about me and Allan gently but firmly putting him in the picture. Although he did not mention Frank, Ronnie wished me whatever my heart desired and asked only that I keep a part of myself, however small, for him to love. I had to smile, for although Ronnie was not the type of man I could have ever

192

imagined myself with, he was at least consistent in the advancing of his affections, and he was kind.

≈⋘

Frank arrived one afternoon as the first green pinheads appeared on the hazel. I saw him from a distance, riding a bicycle up the avenue. I thought later how telling it was that even as a speck so far away, I was sure that it was him. He had taken the train to Kildare and cycled the rest, a journey of nearly forty miles. We went in and I brought him to the little sitting room beside the kitchen where, in winter, seasoned cuts of beech crackled from dawn.

— Mother, this is Frank. A friend from Monument.

— From Monument? Mother turned from her easel. — I have always wanted to paint the quays of Monument.

We had tea and hot scones and, afterwards, Mother showed him her watercolours. Frank said,

— You should exhibit.

— Oh, I never would. Who would buy them?

— I would, if I had the money, he said.

We went walking then, and the evening was the first one in which a real stretch of light was evident. Where we had paused by a stile on the day of the funeral, this time we crossed it into the lake field and walked to a derelict shed where once ewes had been brought with their newborn lambs out of the harsh weather.

We were both so happy that words were unimportant. We didn't even touch, as I recall. It must have been that afternoon that he told me about his family, about his father, a merchant seaman who, like most in his trade, had been put out of work by the war. Frank had been to school and had read the classics. He liked Milton and Wordsworth. He did not intend to spend his whole life working on the docks in Monument, he said, but could see no alternative until after the war.

— After the war, I remember saying to him. — The whole world is waiting until after the war.

We had supper with Mother and, when she went to bed, sat either side of the fire as the silence of the great house in the vast reaches of the echoingly empty countryside seemed to vibrate. I told him about the problems we were having with local land agitators and how only Allan could save Longstead from the Land Commission. Frank was silent for such a long time that I began to wonder if he'd heard what I had said.

— I sometimes think there is no answer, he said eventually.

A log fell out on the hearth and he picked it with the tongs and put it back in place.

— I know people whose minds are filled with nothing but destruction. It's as if they want to erase the past. You can't talk to them. They won't change, he said.

— So there is no hope, I said.

— Sometimes I think the only hope is to get out of Ireland. To get as far away as possible and to love my country from a distance.

I didn't tell him then how I had often felt the same, but as I saw him into Allan's room that night, then went to my own and got into bed, I was lifted up by this great vision of us together somewhere far away, our hearts filled with love and our backs turned forever on destruction.

ॐॐ

Those were the soaring days. I can tell you that I had never lived before then, nor known my own soul. Frank came up from Monument to Meath almost every weekend, or if he didn't, it was because the train to Dublin had been cancelled due to lack of fuel. I got John Rafter to teach me to drive our car so that I could collect him from Kildare station, or if the guards were out, scrutinising the roads for cars not entitled to burn precious fuel, I would meet him at a prearranged point between Longstead and Kildare and he would load his bicycle into the car and we would drive home. One Saturday morning, John Rafter drove up to see if we wanted anything brought to or collected from Dublin. Five minutes later, Frank and I were in the van with him, heading east.

After that, Dublin, less than an hour's drive, was where we most often met. Frank took the train directly and I made my way into the city by means of a lift or the erratic bus service. Mother adapted without demur to our relationship and began to look forward to Frank's visits to Longstead. He was a very good listener; she told him tales from her Yorkshire childhood that I had never heard before.

I came to regard Dublin – its grey streets, its newspaper vendors and ponds of ducks and grimed statues – with the utmost affection, for my baptism of love took place among them all. We walked through St Stephen's Green, arm in arm, or by the Liffey bridges, or sometimes took a tram to Sandymount and walked its vast beach, so far out on occasions that I wondered if we would ever make it back to shore. I didn't care. I sensed that I sailed rather than strolled, that the whole world, hitherto a place of mystery and problems, was embellished richly for my benefit. Each night, I took the bus or, if I was lucky, a lift home, and

195

Frank either came with me or went back directly to Monument.

As the warm days of May came in, we took picnics down to the woods in Longstead and lay there on carpets of bluebells. One day, we went for a spin with Mother in her pony-drawn trap, out the gates of Longstead, through Tirmon and in a loop towards the village of Grange. It was a day of endless promise, the grass banks of the narrow roads shining with primroses and the air rich with their scent. Peace lay on the land like a warm, caring hand.

— Shall we call in on the Penroses? Mother asked as we approached Grange and the walls of Mount Penrose came into view.

— I don't think this would be a good time, Mother, I said.

— Stanley Penrose is one of the best landlords in Ireland, Mother said to Frank.

— Then maybe we should go in and burn the place to the ground, Frank said and nudged me.

— Are you a revolutionary? Mother asked.

— Not really, he said. — I just know one or two.

— I adore revolution, Mother said. — It must be so exciting!

— Well, we're not going to burn Mount Penrose today, Mother, just to amuse you, I said.

— It is completely panelled in oak, Mother observed as we made our way home.

In Longstead that evening, I told Frank about Norman Penrose and how my family's greatest wish was that I would marry him.

— Maybe your family is right, he said.

— I would die, I replied.

— There's a lot to be said for security, Frank said. — For an assured future.

— Look at me, I said, and he did. — I would die, I repeated, and neither of us smiled.

The following weekend we met in Dublin and took a tram out as far as Howth. In warm heather, as yachts like toys glided at our feet, we kissed with a new urgency. And when we got back to Dublin, we went not to the place where the bus left from, but to a hotel called The Wicklow. In the back bar, we drank whiskies, then each of us went, at three-minute intervals, up the curving stairs to the bedroom Frank had reserved.

It was that night that I first felt the all-possessing thrill of love. I felt as if my body had been turned inside out. I wanted to keep the moment for all time, indissoluble.

— Was it bad? he asked afterwards.

I rolled into him. — They say for girls who've ridden horses it's easier.

— I might have known, he said.

❧

Bella came home in May with a man in tow. In his mid-thirties, tall and cool, he was called Nick Sinclair and worked in London in some ministry or other, a family tradition, I gathered. He had never been to Ireland before.

— Iz is the backbone of Longstead, Bella told him.

She was radiant and Nick Sinclair could not drag his eyes from her.

— Wonderful old place, he said.

— What's the latest from Rafter? Bella enquired.

— His son still says that the Land Commission will hold

off until the end of this year, I replied. To Nick I said, —
We all hope that the war will end and our brother Allan
will come home.

Bella described for Nick how Longstead was in peril.

— They just take it?

— They pay for it with pieces of worthless paper called
land bonds. So yes, in effect, they take it, I said.

— Nick says we may not have to wait too long for the
war to end, don't you, darling?

Nick smiled thinly. — Hopefully.

— Nick knows but cannot say, Bella said.

After supper, Bella announced that she and Nick were to
be married. Mother seemed pleased in a glassy-eyed sort of
way. I went to the kitchen and found a bottle of the
champagne left over from Bella's party. We sat and drank as
Bella described how she adored life in London and Nick
made commitments to become better acquainted with
Ireland.

— Is there another bottle of fizz? Bella asked.

— Another?

— I just want to make sure there's one here when you
announce your news, said Bella.

I laughed her off. — I have no news.

She turned to Nick. — There's this wonderful man who
is completely infatuated with our Iz.

— I'm not surprised, said Nick.

— You mean Frank? Mother said.

Bella's face went into spasm. — *Who* did you say?

— Frank, Mother said, with no idea of the consternation
she was causing. — That lovely young man from
Monument. He is quite the connoisseur of art. He very
much admires my birds.

Bella put down her glass. — Are we talking of the *dock worker*? I don't believe this.

— Frank believes in a united Ireland, said Mother, and I agree with him.

— Oh my God! cried Bella and closed her eyes. She turned to Nick. — The man I was *actually* referring to is Norman Penrose. He has taken over the running of our farm and *transformed* it. His uncle is Sir Charles Penrose.

— Ah, Nick said and nodded.

— Iz, Norman Penrose adores you. Are you completely stupid? Bella asked.

I marvelled at my own composure.

— Bella, I am so pleased for your happiness, and for yours, Nick. But since no one bullied you to come to your decision, I'd be grateful if you could bear that in mind when it comes to me.

— I don't believe this, Bella said again.

— I may even hold an exhibition, Mother said, gazing at the tiny bubbles spiralling up from the bottom of her glass.

Later, Bella got me on my own.

— By all means have your fling with your handsome dock man, but, for God's sake, when you come to your senses, marry Norman and save Longstead.

— How dare you speak like that, Bella! Why should I forsake my happiness to suit you? Or anyone else?

— Because the happiness you refer to is an illusion. This is the first man who's managed to lay a hand on you, so of course you like him, but then you have to take a thousand other things into consideration. Such as, who is he? What does he represent? Is his background compatible with our own? Sadly, the answer is no.

—You are despicable!

— I'm a pragmatist. It just won't work and it's my duty as your older sister to tell you.

—You are so stuck in the past that it makes me ill!

— I've spoken to Mother, Bella said quietly. — She told me he's quite the hothead, your docker. Wants to burn down Mount Penrose, she said.

—That was a joke!

— Maybe it wasn't. Nothing would surprise me in this country nowadays. It's being run by corner boys. And dock hands.

I faced her. — I used to worship you, Bella. I used to be so proud to watch you and to have such a beautiful older sister. But what you have just said makes me ashamed that I have ever known you.

My sister set her face at its sharpest. — I'm going to forget that. But believe me when I say this: I have a duty to Daddy and this family that you seem to have decided to ignore and I'm not going to stand to one side and watch my younger sister make a complete fool of herself.

❧

One evening as we sat by the fire, Mother suddenly put her book down.

— Iz, I want to go home, she said.

My first thought was, *She's losing her mind.*

—You are at home, Mother.

She sighed. — I want to go home to Yorkshire.

I saw her, the ghost of a tall, pretty woman, sitting before me like a child.

—Why?

— It's time.

I made us a pot of tea. Ever since Daddy's death, she said, she had thought about returning to Yorkshire, where some of her cousins still lived and where there was a house left to her by her stepfather. It was, she said, despite all the years in County Meath, the place she loved most and whenever she woke up and imagined for the briefest moment that she was a child again in Yorkshire, she was happiest.

— Of course you must go, if that's what you wish, I said.

— Might you come with me, Iz?

— I don't think so, Mother, I said gently.

She smiled. — That's all right, I understand. I didn't think you would.

I wrote at her request to a land agent in Skipton who managed the house and told him that she would be taking it over. In the context of Longstead's problems, it seemed like a very sensible decision.

❧❦

Although Ireland was neutral and although the most all-engulfing war the world had ever known was referred to in Ireland as 'the Emergency', ours was a benign and knowing neutrality, so that when, on June 7th, all the newspapers carried banner headlines announcing the invasion of Europe, there was a lift in everyone's step. We in Ireland knew that only when the war was won would shortages ease and the full benefits of being independent begin to be exploited.

But there were those who were determined, against all

the odds, to strike against what they saw as the remnants of imperialism. A week after D–Day, I read of an attack on a lonely police barracks in Munster and the death of a garda sergeant. Subversives were responsible, the paper said, reporting that the Minister for Justice had vowed to hunt down the killers without mercy and to bring them to account.

Allan wrote from France and his letter did the rounds of everyone in Longstead. He had come in with the first landings. He was well, Hitler was beaten and the war would be over by Christmas, Allan said. I brought his letter down to the village and read it to the Rafters.

— Thanks be to God, Mr Rafter said.

— I'll see the word gets around, Iz, said John, the son, and nodded reassuringly.

It was turning into a good summer from the point of view of fattening cattle and saving hay. Norman had been in one part of Longstead or another almost every day, directing teams of men in their tasks. In late June, the hay had been drawn into the barns near the house and also into a hay shed renovated by Norman for the purpose, which stood by a boundary wall not far from the village. But one morning in early July, one of our farm hands came in, wide eyed.

— The new barn, Miss … I knew what he was going to tell me. The look of fear in his face was the worst part. — They burned it to the ground.

It was the waste I found most distressing, for I too had helped in the fields, bringing out flasks of tea and bread and working until ten at night to get the hay saved. Forty cattle could have wintered off what had been destroyed. Although people in Tirmon must have seen the blaze, since they lived the other side of the wall, no one had raised the alarm or tried to help.

Word of Longstead's problems travelled fast. Among the first to drive up our avenue and show solidarity were Stanley and Norman Penrose.

— It is an outrage, Stanley said, many times. — I have taken the liberty of writing to the government minister who is supposed to be in charge of law and order in this country, expressing my fears for the future of the Free State if this sort of behaviour is allowed to go unpunished.

The day was close and a heaviness lay on the fields and in ditches. While Mother was forced to drink tea with Stanley, Norman asked to walk with me down the avenue.

— You have been on my mind, Ismay, he said, swinging his blackthorn stick.

I thought of Frank and of the evening we had had together in Dublin the week before, walking the streets and listening to the cries of the newspaper vendors.

— I would be less than honest if I did not admit that I admire you greatly.

— I'm sorry?

— It's not as if we haven't known each other since we were children. I would try, with all my power, to give you whatever your heart desired.

The sense of his words came to me gradually, like the growing beat of drums.

— I mean it. I have never meant anything as much.

— This is inappropriate, I said.

— I know what your concerns must be, but I have tried to anticipate them. My father wants to live in Dublin. He says the winters down here no longer suit his chest. Mount Penrose will be ours entirely. There is a lovely small house on the grounds which I will adapt for Mrs Seston. She will be comfortable and all her needs looked after. Until your brother comes home, I will continue, at no charge whatsoever, to manage and maintain Longstead. Despite the outrage that has just taken place, I believe it will be far more difficult, if not impossible, for the agitators to succeed against Longstead if they see me involved as, so to speak, a member of the family.

I stared at him.

Norman continued, — I have, if I can be permitted to speak on my own behalf, a good sense of judgement in these matters.

I began to run back up the avenue. I never looked back. I saw my mother by the hall door with Stanley Penrose, her face vacant, his stern. I ran on, into our walled apple orchard where fruit was budding. I wanted Frank. His voice, his hands. I wanted us to fly away beyond the grasp of all the forces that were trying to wrench us asunder. Why was I the one who could not love the man of her choice? What I was caught up in, I dimly understood, was the embodiment of history. But history was what I most feared.

ৡৄ৺

I sat up in bed in The Wicklow and looked at seagulls on nearby ridges. Dublin was teeming with country people up for the Dublin Horse Show. I had met Frank the night before and we had not yet left the room. I relished the crisp sheets and the sheer dryness of the hotel compared to Longstead.

—What are you thinking about? I asked.

—You, he said. — Me and you.

The night before, I had thought that tiredness was the cause of a new seriousness in him, but now it was evident again. I stroked his chest.

—You're worried about something.

He smiled. — Me? I'm not a worrier.

—Tell me what's the matter.

He grinned and tried to shrug it off. But then his chin went down. — It's not really my problem.

— Go on.

— Do you remember that business near Cork back in June? A garda sergeant was shot.

— I read about it, yes.

— Stephen asked me to cover for him, Frank said.

I sat up. — And did you?

Frank nodded. — The guards came to our house and I swore to them that Stephen had been with me all that night.

— My God, Frank. And he hadn't?

— I made it all up. I never saw him that night.

A droning inevitability made it hard to hear. — Did he murder the guard? I asked quietly.

— I've never asked and even if I had, he wouldn't tell me.

— And yet you lied.

— He is my friend.

We lay there, suddenly cold.

— If the guards find out I lied, I'll be lifted on suspicion and interned. But the people Stephen is tied up with are even more dangerous. If I hadn't lied, I could have been shot.

I could scarcely breathe. — And is it over now, or will they do something else?

— It's never over, he said.

— But you – it's nothing to do with you!

He closed his eyes. — They get you into something, like misleading the guards, then they use it, they twist and twist.

No time existed between my understanding the nature of his position and my decision. I got out of bed and began to dress.

— We're getting out, I said. — We're leaving. The war doesn't have to be over for us to go to England.

He sighed. — You can't do that. You can't walk away from Longstead and leave everything behind.

— That's exactly what I'm going to do, I said.

— What about your mother? She's a lovely woman. You can't leave her.

— Mother is going to live in Yorkshire.

It began to rain and the beak of a big seagull outside gleamed with wetness.

— I have nothing, Frank said. — Just what you see now. No land, no house, no money. Nothing.

I came around and sat on the bed beside him. — You have you and that's all I want.

— No one will approve.

— To hell with them! We'll make our own life. We'll go to England and then, after Christmas, when the war is won, we'll go to … I don't know, Australia. Someplace no one knows us.

He laughed and gathered me to him. — You're crazy, he said.

— You'll be safe there. It will be as if these problems never existed.

He looked out over the rooftops. — That would be a dream.

— You've got to live your dreams, I said. — No one else will do that for you.

He nodded slowly. — Then that's what we'll do. We'll live our dream.

— When?

— As soon as we can. A couple of weeks.

I kissed him as though I could never kiss him enough, or again. I wished we could go to sleep in that little room, warm and safe, and that, when we woke, we would be in a place where our dreams would begin.

❧

Three days later, a letter arrived from Bella.

Darling Iz,

This has to be brief, because Nick says I must be careful about what I put down on paper.

Please, please believe me when I say that the person you are seeing is HIGHLY UNSUITABLE. I implore you to believe me. Nick has contacts who have told him that EVERY MOVE-MENT IS BEING WATCHED. The person in question is EXTREMELY DANGEROUS. So if our friendship stands for anything, just trust me in what I say.

Your loving sister,

Bella

Sick with fear for what might be about to happen to Frank, I walked into the village. We had arranged to meet in a week's time in Dublin, at Kingsbridge railway station, and to go from there on the night mail boat to London. In the post office in Tirmon I filled out a telegram form: COME UP URGENT IZ.

Then I remembered Bella's letter. *Every movement is being watched.* I felt the eyes of the postmistress, into whose hands I was about to entrust the telegram. She lived in the house at the end of the village nearest to where our barn had been set alight. I suddenly understood the power of the alliances drawn up against us: those who wanted to grab Longstead; the Land Commission; their acquiescent allies in the public service, such as the woman in this post office; and now the guards, not to mention the IRA. I crumpled the form, threw it in a wastepaper basket, then realising what I had done, retrieved it and left the tiny shop and its open-mouthed custodian.

That afternoon, although our fuel was scarce and kept for dire emergencies, I took the car out and drove towards Dublin. I was terrified. I was sure that Bella had made the situation far worse for Frank with her enquiries. But if his every movement was being watched, then a telegram to him would be intercepted. In a post office in a tiny village on the outskirts of Dublin, I sent a telegram to Tom King, c/o Monumentals rugby club, with the message COME TO LONGSTEAD SOONEST IZ.

I had no idea if it would be delivered. At home, exhausted beyond utterance, I went to bed and lay there, shaking, wondering what we had done to deserve the wrath of the world.

❦

It was lunchtime the next day when I heard the car on the avenue. I hurried out and Tom was standing there, his big, freckled face anxious. I was so afraid that the guards or Bella or the IRA might arrive and find him that I made him put the car in a shed, then brought him down to the lake field where no one could see us.

— What's going on, Iz?

— I think something dreadful has happened, I said and told him about Bella and Nick.

— Jesus, Tom said and rubbed his face. — That's just what he needs.

Across the lake, the stands of beech had begun the first phase of their turning. On the near shore, a heron only needed to spread its wings to become airborne.

— Is he all right? I asked.

— He's agitated, Tom said.

— We're going to England.

— I know. He's working double time trying to get as much money together as he can.

— Could he not just go to the guards and tell them the truth?

— He could, Tom said, but he could end up swinging for it. A guard was shot. Frank covered up for Stephen and that makes him an accessory to murder.

— Why did he do it? I asked. — Why did he put his life in danger?

— He grew up beside Stephen, Tom said. — They're like brothers. And in more ways than one. You see, Stephen is almost family there.

It took me a moment to work it out, but then I suddenly remembered Alice's fierceness as she had tried to go to Stephen's rescue at the dance.

— Alice, I said.

Tom nodded. — Alice and Stephen, he said. — How could Frank have not covered for him?

So much I didn't know, and yet I clung to the image of us sailing away, leaving all this behind. A covey of doves flew over our heads, banking sharply.

— Please go back to Monument and tell him what I've told you, I said. — And tell him that I'll be in Kingsbridge at the agreed time, but not next week. Tomorrow.

The Misses Carr owned a fishing lodge on a lake in County Cavan and had invited Mother there. She left that evening in John Rafter's van, her hat askew, her painting equipment stowed in a picnic hamper. I could do nothing about the shock she would get when she returned and found me gone. But, I reasoned, she and I would soon be separated anyway. As for Longstead, the staff would look after it until Allan came home but, in the meantime, it would be managed by Bella or Harry. In fact, Bella's fiancé's political connections would be put to better use in persuading the Land Commission to leave us alone than in persecuting the man I loved.

It was Bella I wrote to in the end, explaining what I was doing and why. I gave her no clue as to where we were going and, the next morning I left the letter on the hall table, then with a small suitcase, drove as far as Grange, where I caught the bus.

In their inexorable changing, the deep, autumn colours of the countryside matched how I felt. All my childhood, I had been used to going away, and although this was more final, Ireland too would eventually change for the better, I knew, and one day we could come back.

The bus left me by Nelson's Pillar and I began the walk towards the quays which led to Kingsbridge. We had agreed five o'clock and it was now just after three. I knew from my school trips that the boats left around seven. Wind blew in from the sea and made tiny waves on the surface of the Liffey. I could imagine him in his railway carriage, now steaming through County Kildare, checking his watch and looking for the first sight of Dublin.

A train stood at a platform in Kingsbridge, sending out massive explosions of steam that gathered like rain clouds in the span of the vaulted roof. Passengers hurried to board and whistles sounded. I found the platform where the train from Monument was expected and stood there, near the buffers, my eyes on the curve of the track, half a mile away.

I thought about Bella and her ability for destruction and wondered, when all was said and done, if she would ever know the happiness that I had found. It was not that I wished her any less, and not so long before I would have worried for her, but I could not understand how two sisters as we were could in such a fundamental way be so different.

I saw the steam first. It obscured the bend on which my eyes were locked, but then the chimney of the train appeared and it whistled gladly, like a horse that knows it is home. It came in surrounded by its own noise and steam and shuddered to a halt ten yards from where I stood. Steam wafted over the platform and the disembarking passengers loomed out of it like ghosts. I could always make him out from a distance and now strained to see him before he saw me. The passengers were handing their tickets to a collector and filing out past me. I looked in every face, then beyond them. I saw a tall figure hand a ticket to the collector. I suddenly felt my legs go funny. She walked towards me.

— Do you remember me? Alice said.

A coal fire burned in the station bar. I had told her I didn't want a drink, but she went anyway and ordered two glasses of brandy. I was weak with terror.

—Where's Frank? I asked when she sat down again.

— Drink the brandy.

— Now where is he? Has he been arrested? *Where is he?*

— Frank is gone, Iz, she said.

I shook my head. —You mean gone ahead.

— I mean gone. He's gone. He's not coming back, she said.

— But that's impossible, I said. — He and I are going away together.

She looked at me coldly and I then remembered the night of the dance, when we had been introduced and how she had looked at me in the same way. She said,

— It wouldn't have worked. Believe me, it never does.

I stared at her. —What are you talking about?

—Too big a difference, she said, the two sides don't mix.

— What do you know about us? I cried. —You know nothing. I want to know where Frank has gone!

She looked away, as if I lacked sense, then she took a drink. — I'm sorry, but how could he ever trust you after what has happened? Your sister tried to turn the law on him.

—You think I had something to do with that? It was I who warned him about it! Why are you saying this? I cried.

—You've no notion, do you? she said. —You think that

people like you, with your land and your fine ways, can just stoop down and pick one of us up when it suits you?

— You have absolutely no idea what you're talking about, I said. I was shaking with fear.

Her face seemed to soften. — He did what he did as much out of concern for you as for his own safety. It was a hard decision, but Frank made it. He didn't want both of your lives to be ruined.

— I don't believe he said that, I said.

— He did give me a message for you.

I wanted to stand up and run away from her, but I couldn't. — What?

— He said to tell you to live your dream.

CHAPTER SIXTEEN

1944–45

Winter entombed the midlands. Mother was so cold that her bed and wardrobe were moved downstairs to the little sitting room where a fire was kept going around the clock. Except for those in the kitchen, every window was permanently iced up and no water came from taps or flowed in the toilet. The electricity failed for days at a time and we reverted to the Longstead of my childhood, of trimming the wicks of oil lamps and of candles. The wireless no longer worked. Outside, wind whipped snow into massive drifts which threatened to further engulf the house. I kept warm most days by shovelling. Even if we'd had fuel for the car, we could not have gone anywhere, as whole sections of Meath and Kildare were cut off. John Rafter came up the avenue with provisions and the post; he sat in the kitchen and I made him tea. The whole country was prey to widespread hardship and trouble, he told me.

— What kind of trouble? I asked.

— You know, Iz, he said. — There's some lads out there that'll never stop until they get a bullet.

In the early days, I did not think that I could live. As Frank had introduced me to the meaning of love, so had I come to learn grief from him as well. I understood then what Mother was going through, for we had both lost someone we loved. Grief clung to me, and if moments of brief respite occurred, when the crushing reality resumed, it was always worse.

I could not understand what had happened. Our plans had been so clear, the dangers we were escaping so manifest. I could only imagine that, in the end, Bella's intervention had been decisive for him, that the sheer scale of what we would have to overcome seemed too much. And yet, up till then, I would have bet everything that no scale was too much for him, he who always emerged from the fiercest mêlée with the ball in his hands.

But as the days towards Christmas wore on and I heard nothing from him, in order to preserve my own sanity and my dignity, I had to accept the possibility that I had made a mistake. I had been prepared to risk everything, but he had not. What lack this arose from in him, I couldn't say, except that it must have come ultimately from a deficit of courage in the one area in which I would have sworn that he was peerless. And then I thought of his sister, and the crooked brace of prejudice in which her thoughts were formed, and I accepted with dismay that in the end, history had won out. It was cruel, for it called into question the value of every moment we had enjoyed.

I set about forgetting him. My letter to Bella, which had never been sent but which for some reason I had kept, now seemed like part of someone else's story. It was easier if I persuaded myself that, in truth, I had been lucky to escape. This did not liberate my soul, just deadened it.

❧

We had been invited to Mount Penrose for Christmas, but Mother was relieved when I suggested we stay at home. Still, Norman Penrose was one of the very few who made the journey up our avenue – on the pretext of checking the farm. He came in and stood in front of the fire and drank tea laced with whiskey. I made sure that Mother stayed put on these occasions, for I would not have been able for Norman on his own. And yet, there was an inexorability about him that led me, despite myself, to go to bed some nights thinking the unthinkable.

I considered running away, but there was still a war on and one could go nowhere. We had no money coming in and the bank had begun writing us stiff letters. The staff at Longstead, or what few remained, knew the dire situation, but at least in Longstead they had a roof over their heads and the produce, however disorganised, of a 1,500-acre farm. Although the war was as good as won, it still hung over us even on a good day, we who lived in a country that was meant to be at peace.

A week after Christmas, John Rafter delivered a box of provisions which I brought to the kitchen and unpacked. The box was lined with newspaper. Something caught my eye. I removed the paper from the box and smoothed it out. I had to sit down to steady myself. A man and a woman stared out from their photographs beneath black headlines. The paper was three weeks old. The couple had been shot dead in an ambush in Tipperary by armed members of the detective bureau. Both had been members of the IRA. His name was Stephen Duggan. Hers was Alice Waters.

꙳

As if a trowel had been taken to where my recent grief had been heeled in, now it was laid bare again without remorse. It was not just that death seemed so near, or so shocking, but that life itself suddenly seemed so trivial. Overwhelming, too, was the feeling that I was so utterly marginal to important events. I, who thought she had been at the centre of developments, learned of them only weeks in arrears from discarded newspapers.

I wondered if Frank's picture had appeared in some newspaper or other and if he too was dead or just locked in a jail. He might well have been, for all we knew in Longstead. I grieved then, not just for him again, but for his sister and for Stephen Duggan, a man I had seen just once. I had been foolish to think that the wedge driven by centuries between our different classes could be removed by something as insubstantial as love.

I thought much of love during those days and came to see it as just an ideal that men strove for, like truth or liberty, unattainable in any absolute sense. One man's truth was another's lie and what was freedom to one was slavery to the next. Life was about survival, about using what you had to your best advantage and in not throwing away everything in a moment of madness.

I came in at noon one day in mid-January and saw the pile of unopened post lying on the table in the breakfast room. I had begun collecting the bills and other pieces of business correspondence, since if they went through Mother's hands they invariably disappeared, and letters concerning Daddy's estate which a solicitor in Navan was dealing with. I sat down and began to slit open all the envelopes. When I lifted the last one, I saw the telegram. It lay there in its green buff with the utmost sinisterness. I realised a number of things at once: that Mother must have taken separate delivery of the telegram and decided not to open it; that she must then have hidden it beneath the pile of letters, knowing that I would discover it. I realised then too that the entire house was hushed. Listening. Waiting for me to come in here and do what Mother had been unable to do. What else do I remember? I'll tell you what – the silence of death that lay everywhere, at whose centre I stood.

❧

We had no one to bury, for Allan was never found. The beautiful, clear-eyed boy who loved his horses and his fishing and who would come home and put everything to rights had been obliterated by a mine. I remember little of the next days, just that my body seemed like a well ever primed by grief. I wept without cease.

At the memorial service, I heard only every other word from our rector, a tired-looking man who spoke of love and suffering and compassion. I wanted him to say how justice lacked in even the most fundamental sense, about the basic unfairness in nature and, if he existed at all, which I doubted, of God's unremitting cruelty. God seemed to have us singled out for the most heartless of his games. But our game was now as good as over. I knew what had to be done.

Bella, married and pregnant, arrived home with Nick. Harry came from London and Lolo drove down from Fermanagh with her husband. Our allies gathered from every corner of Ireland, some of whom I had never seen before and, in all likelihood, never would again, but they had been galvanised into action despite fuel rationing, floods and great distance, as if our shoring up was a sudden but vital campaign in the survival of our kind. They were of all ages and frequently bizarre in appearance, centuries mattering little for changes in dress or deportment, and almost all of them were determined to display that shining, outward resilience and imperviousness to grief which is the traditional hallmark of the colonist. From Monument came the Shaws, Ronnie's parents, a lopsided, always half-smiling man and a big, angular woman who introduced herself as Peppy.

— Ronnie knows, dear. He's devastated, she said and kissed my cheek, although it was the freezing cold tip of her big nose that I felt most. — He wants you to know you're in his thoughts constantly.

— I'm glad he's well, I said.

— Ronnie is like his father. He'll enjoy himself wherever he goes, even during a war, she said. — Do you know that when his regiment shipped out for France, he brought two sets of hunting boots, trees intact?

I smiled.

— Ronnie was right, Peppy said. — You're divine.

— How is ... Monument? I asked, unable to stop myself.

Peppy Shaw's pale eyes were flecked at their centres with shards of knowing grey.

— Some people don't seem to understand that their particular war has long been won, she said quietly. —

There's no need of guns and bullets. They who once ruled are finished, by which I mean 'we'. This is the country of young Ireland now and time is all that is needed for it to come of age.

Our tragedy had cut through local politics too, it seemed, for men from all parties assembled at our church, and even though it was forbidden by their own religion, many of them came inside. Later, the house was thronged and warm and people shouted to be heard. Mother sat, mute, as though winded by a fall, the Misses Carr, disconcerting replicas, either side of her.

— Iz, we must talk.

One would have liked to say how pregnancy suited Bella, how she had bloomed; alas, her bump looked more like an impediment which she was powerless to navigate. We went upstairs to what was still referred to as Bella's bedroom. Lolo, poor, dear Lolo, had begun to resemble Daddy in the way she scowled, closed the door. Bella said, — He has been mentioned in dispatches.

— That's a huge thing, Harry said. — It's like a decoration.

How superfluous the term *decoration*, I thought.

— Mother has no idea, Lolo said.

— I think she understands more than all of us, I said.

Harry stood, hands in his pockets, looking out the bedroom window. — I saw you speaking to Rafter, he said to Bella.

— Mr Rafter is the best friend we have, Bella said, avoiding my amused look. — He has told me exactly where we stand. He says it's now a matter of weeks rather than months. Unless there are developments.

— I thought the fact they had all come to pay their respects rather meant that we had escaped all that, Lolo said.

— Just means they were using the opportunity to sneak a look at their new property, said Bella dryly.

— What developments has Rafter in mind? Harry enquired.

Bella lifted her chin. — Longstead is lost unless Iz marries Norman Penrose.

They turned as one to me, but I had made my mind up and was ready for them. I just smiled.

— The Penroses can do no wrong in these people's eyes, Bella said. — If Iz marries Norman, then Longstead will not be touched. The Land Commission will back off. Mr Rafter says he can as good as guarantee that that is what will happen.

They all looked to me again.

— Do you *want* to marry Norman, Iz? asked Lolo.

— I'll marry him, I said.

Harry's breath came out in a long, relieved hiss. — Well, were it not for the occasion, I'd suggest we drink champagne, he grinned.

— Thank God. I'll tell Rafter, Bella said.

They came and kissed me in turn. Bella and I left the bedroom last.

— By the way, on the matter of you know who … she began.

— Please.

— Thank *God* Nick made enquiries. It seems he is on a list of the most wanted men in Ireland, she said.

— I don't wish to discuss it.

— He's got a price on his head, you know.

— *I don't wish to discuss it!* I screamed and left her there, her front jutting out like an anthill.

᳗

My engagement to Norman did not have the effect of stopping the land agitation completely. Some local people who owed nothing to the Penroses felt that a great prize was being snatched from them and continued to lobby and to hold meetings and to demand action from their local representatives.

Although the outcome of the war was no longer in doubt, I felt as if I were in my own war where survival depended on hard decisions and compromises. I saw Norman at least every Sunday, either when Mother and I went for luncheon to Mount Penrose or when Norman and his father came to us. I wore an engagement ring that had been his mother's and we went for walks, during which he spoke in steady tones about his ambitions and plans for Longstead. He had placed a notice announcing our engagement in the national newspapers. He had planned an engagement party, the first party in Mount Penrose in fifty years, he said. Although we had not yet been intimate, Norman seemed to already regard me as his wife.

I spent most of February clearing the detritus of winter from the shrubberies and digging beds in preparation for spring vegetables. I worked often without pause for four or five hours, as if afraid that stopping would give me time to think. I organised the annual spring clean of Longstead, the most thorough in memory, and helped carry out carpets and rugs onto the gravel and went back in to inspect, with dismay, the gaping holes in our floors where rot had thrived uninterrupted for fifty years. Norman sent over a carpenter and within two weeks new timbers had been laid and varnished.

—These windows are all beyond repair, Norman said.—We'll have to replace them.

I did not protest. It seemed easier just to let him get on with it.

The party was held in Mount Penrose on a Saturday in late February, when gales ripped the length of Ireland. Bella and Nick arrived home, Bella now hugely pregnant and exhausted from a nine-hour sea crossing. They were well suited, Nick and Bella, she with her imperious demeanour and he with the kind of icy authority that sits on men who see their wishes enacted as laws. Mother's stated intentions about her repatriation to Yorkshire were ignored by Bella, who advised that they were nothing more but the onset of dotage.

On the evening of the party, I put on a dress that had been made for me in Dublin and would eventually be paid for out of Daddy's meagre estate. It was silk crepe, the colour of sunset, and fell from beneath a bow at the waist in tiers. The neck was square cut and the top half broken only by a single row of buttons. Nick drew in his breath when I came downstairs.

—You look absolutely ravishing, he said and kissed my cheek.

We left Mother playing whist with Mrs Rainbow and set out in John Rafter's van for Grange. As gusts of wind struck the little vehicle and tried to fling it off the road, I made lists in my head of the things I would prefer to be doing rather than going to my engagement party. Halfway to Grange, I lost count and abandoned the exercise.

Mount Penrose was a square, severe house and had been built in the mid-nineteenth century when the fashion must have been for oak: staircases, doors, window reveals, floors, fireplaces and skirting boards all brooded the provenance of dark forests. I thought of our own home, ramshackle in comparison, yet in its own way comfortable. The Penroses had installed an orchestra and although the country was still on war rations, one hundred people would eat roast beef and drink champagne. Norman met me at the door and I took his arm and we went in. A man with a black moustache came towards us, limping.

— I now know I was wrong, he said. — You are not just the most beautiful woman in Meath, but in Ireland.

— Ronnie! I laughed and he hugged me. — I thought you were somewhere in France!

— Got in the way of a Gerry bullet, I'm afraid, Ronnie said, but they didn't realise they were dealing with a Monumentals man.

He grinned and the gap between his front teeth appeared and made me laugh out loud. Perhaps it was the moustache, but he seemed older and in the process more dignified. I wanted to ask what had become of Frank, but Bella and Nick were hovering. Then I saw Ronnie's cufflinks in the shape of rugby balls and the thought of the evening on which he had been presented with them made me plunge.

Except for the beginning of war, nothing is headier than the prospect of its ending: people spoke of curtailments being suspended in a month, of travel restrictions being abolished and of sons coming home. As the band struck up, Stanley Penrose swung me around the floor of his hall, his white whiskers tickling my chin, and confidently predicted that I would give him at least four grandchildren. He pressed me on the date for the wedding, but when I was evasive showed a flash of the steel with which he had made his fortune.

— You're not going to go on playing the monkey with the poor lad, are ye now? he asked.

— I beg your pardon?

— You know what I mean, Miss.

I excused myself and went and locked myself into the Penrose's toilet. I looked in the gilt-framed mirror and saw my lovely dress and my anxious face. I will do this, I told myself, and went back out.

I danced with twenty men and each one vied with his predecessor to assure me of my destined happiness. I was terrified: of Stanley Penrose, of these people, this house. I looked around for Ronnie, but each time I saw him, I was grabbed anew and steered for the music.

Norman and I sat down with Bella and Nick for supper. My future husband, although he would never entirely shed his solemn demeanour, even on a night such as this, nonetheless was lighter than I had ever seen him. I tried to let go and to imagine the fine life that awaited me here, the wealth and the certainty. Norman's father called the party to order and proposed our toast, which involved him making a long and serious speech about land agitation, during which everyone shouted *Hear! Hear!* and nodded their heads grimly as their host spoke of the shortcomings of the government, the injustice of the law and the brink of anarchy on which he assured us we were all poised. Norman replied briefly and then everyone stood up and applauded me. Led by Norman to the centre of the floor, we danced for them in the house of which I would soon be mistress and all I could think of was the dance in the hotel in Monument.

— I have had a room made up here for you tonight, Norman said with great weight.

— Here?

— In your new home.

— Oh.

— It will be the first time a woman has slept here since my mother died. You will be taking her place, he said.

Hot and a little dizzy, I went outside and lit a cigarette. The storm had suddenly died and a moon had come out. I could see John Rafter, also smoking, standing in the field beside his van.

— John?

— How's it going, Iz?

— I'd like you to drive me home.

Feral eyes floated from hedgerows as the van weaved the lanes between Grange and Tirmon. I was chilled although I had done little else but dance.

— Are you all right? John asked.

— I'm just a little tired.

— You're shivering, he said and reached into the back and handed me over a jacket which I put around my shoulders. When he dropped me at Longstead, he said, — I'll go back and wait for Bella and her old fella.

The house was already asleep. How I relished its softness and disorder, its lack of purpose or ambition. I went in and put on the lights in the hall and found a pair of outdoor shoes and a coat, then went outside to the wall beyond the lawn and lit up a last cigarette. How many times I had observed Longstead from that spot, seeing but unseen. My smoke eddied in the night air and I batted it away. Bella and Nick would be home soon and if they found me up, Bella would be full of awkward questions about my leaving my own party so early. There was a noise. I turned. As I did, I was clamped at the mouth and around my waist.

We fell back and I saw the stars reeling. I tried to shout for help. I was pinned and could feel the strength of my attacker and hear him grunting as he held me. I kicked and bit. I could think only of the land agitators, the dispossessed, now come to remove their last remaining obstacle to Longstead. My throat cut. I bit again. Hard.

— *Iz!*

He had released me.

— Jesus, but you can put up a fight! Frank gasped.

CHAPTER SEVENTEEN

1945

His face flitted in and out of shadow as clouds ran across the moon. He was unshaven and his clothes were wet and bedraggled. My first thought was that Bella and Nick would return at any moment.

— Quickly, I said and caught his arm.

I led him down the avenue, across the stile and into the lake field. I took off my shoes, hoisted my dress and ran, my legs drenched from the dew. The moonlight was eerie and erratic and each time it shone I kept thinking it was the lights of the van. Inside the old lambing shed, the floor was covered with the musty hay of former seasons.

— Why …? I began, but I couldn't finish the question, nor did I need to.

He shook his head and I could see in a beam of moonlight how thin he was.

— It was Alice, he said softly. — Had to be.

— She told me … she told me that you'd said you didn't want both our lives to be ruined, I said.

Frank's eyes closed. — I sent her to Dublin to bring you back down with her. I thought it would be safer to cross to England from Monument. She came home and said that you had broken it off with me, that you'd decided it was for the best.

My chest hurt where my breath was caught. — Why?

— Because she was crazy, which is a terrible thing to say about your own sister when she's dead. Because she thought I was betraying what she stood for.

His head was down and his hair fell forward.

— Are you on the run from the guards? I asked.

He nodded.

— And yet you came back for me, I said.

— Tom sent me the notice of your engagement, he said.

— I knew that wasn't what you wanted, because you told me. I knew then that Alice had told me lies.

We kissed in that damp little shed, although I didn't care if the heavens opened.

— I love you, he said. — I will die if I can't be with you.

He unbuttoned my dress, then kissed my shoulders and gently pulled down each strap of my white slip. Unclipping my hair, he smoothed it out with his fingers. I undid his shirt and saw bruising on his shoulder. His chest hairs were darker than those on his head, spreading out before diving in an ever darkening line. I could feel blood I had forgotten surging powerfully, my ears humming and my whole head resonating. Afterwards, I stroked his back and tasted his skin.

— What will become of us? I asked.

— We will become like the stars in the sky, he said.

— The ancient Greeks used to think the stars were their gods.

— Then I want to be Hector, son of Apollo, he said.

— Hector, the great warrior, the greatest in Troy, I said and hugged him close. — My Hector.

Frank said, — I want to do this for the rest of our lives.

I came down to breakfast, my feet barely touching the ground. All night in bed, or what part of it I spent there, I could inhale his skin from mine.

— What on earth came over you last night? Bella asked. — Poor Norman was crestfallen. I had to make your excuses.

— I was feeling ill.

— Perhaps you should see a doctor, said Nick, and as always when he spoke, I felt a chill on my neck.

— I'm perfectly well now, thank you, I said and cut myself a slice of soda bread.

— Stanley Penrose took me aside last night, said Bella, eyeing me. — He thinks it's only reasonable that you give Norman a firm date for your wedding.

— Did he indeed?

— I must say I do think the poor man has a point.

He's far from poor, I wanted to say, but instead I said, — I know. It was unfair of me. I'll decide a date with Norman before the end of this week.

— Well, at least that's something, Bella said and she and Nick exchanged a look.

As if the storms had swept away the final traces of winter, heat poured from the sun, birds sang and darkness and menace were forgotten. Light was exquisite in the garden, illuminating the heads of snowdrops. The love that ran through me, that was my blood, made me want to shout for joy and tell everyone what I was doing. Fifty yards from the house, under a monkey puzzle tree, I sat and made myself remember all the good that had unfolded here, the fine lives that had had this place at their beginning, the great hopes that Longstead had given rise to.

— You're singing.

I whirled. Nick had materialised behind me.

— Oh!

— It was lovely, he said. — Sorry, did I startle you?

— No. I mean, a bit. I was miles away.

— Anywhere in particular? He seemed to radiate a power that threatened everything I wanted. — Bella and I are taking a picnic down the fields and were wondering if you'd like to join us?

He was smiling, but his eyes were too knowing, as if my mind could conceal none of its plans.

— I ... I can't today, thanks. But maybe another day.

— What's happening today?

— I thought ... that I would go and see Norman ... and plan the date for our wedding.

— Now *there's* a good idea, Nick said and strode away down the lawn, hands behind his back.

I would have liked to have had Mother to myself for the morning, but Bella and Nick were always in the room.

— I must get a photograph of you girls, Nick said.

We stood at the front door, Mother in her black straw hat, Bella in the centre, and me. Nick peered down into his box camera.

— Lovely, he said and I heard the clock in the hall strike noon.

Bella went to the kitchen to see what had become of

their picnic and Mother took her easel and pallet to the lawn. I helped her carry her paints and her chair. We went to a spot to the right of the avenue, from which the shining lake could be seen in the distance. Nick and Bella were making their way down to the stile. Even this far away, I could hear Bella's voice.

—You're very good to me, Mother said as I put the chair down.

— It's not difficult when you love someone very much, I said.

— Oh, I do understand how you must go, Iz, but I wish you didn't have to, Mother said.

I stared at her, as if she too, and perhaps all the world, knew my mind.

— Go?

— To live in Mount Penrose, Mother said. — Longstead is so much prettier.

I put my cheek to hers and my arms around her neck. — I will always love you, wherever I am, I said and made my way back inside.

At half past twelve, I walked down the avenue with only the clothes on my back. I could never have foreseen that I would be leaving Longstead without a solitary possession, but that too felt good and uplifting in the way I imagined pilgrims or hermits must feel uplifted as they cast off all in pursuit of a higher goal. I waved to Mother, but she didn't see me. I called,

— Goodbye.

When I reached the gates, I was out of breath, although I had made a point of not hurrying. The village of Tirmon, whether on mornings of icy sleet or as now, when the sun bathed it in almost beatific light, showed few signs that people lived there. I passed Mr Rafter's shop. The clock inside showed ten to one. Scents of coffee and jute sacking followed me along the footpath. I began to sink, unaccountably, as if scents alone could unlock the responsible part of my reasoning process. Turning back, I ran into the shop.

Bells chimed and faces looked up from behind counters. It was one of the small miracles of life that Mr Rafter, despite all his business interests and the need to be in so many different places at once, was nonetheless always in his shop when he was needed.

— Miss, he said. — Have you heard the news?

I felt the familiar internal plunge as dismay overcame hope.

— Oh, God, what?

— The Ruskies are heading for Berlin, Mr Rafter grinned. — It's as good as over.

I closed my eyes with relief. — I didn't know what you were going to tell me.

Mr Rafter's girth, so often derided and sniggered at, was all at once so very replete and comforting. I said,

— The reason I've come in is that I wanted to say that I'd be … most grateful if you could keep an eye on Mother. If anything should ever happen to me, Mr Rafter.

The grocer's clever eyes seemed to join the ranks of all those who could read my intentions.

— And what could happen to you, Iz? he asked quietly.

— I don't expect anything to happen. It's just that, well, you've always been such a friend, I thought that if …

He ran his hand over his face and rubbed his nose vigorously. — Your father and I were the best of friends. We'd talk about history and how each of us had got to where we were. We knew the changes that were coming, we just didn't know when.

— Mother wants to go back to England. Now that the war is nearly over, she'll soon be able to.

— We'll all be sorry to see her go.

— I'm sorry, Mr Rafter. I'm meeting someone, I've got to rush, I said, cursing myself for having come in.

— Ah, you were always the best of them as far as I was ever concerned, he said and walked with me to the door. — But you're far too young to be worrying.

— I know, I said. — I'm sorry.

He held the door for me. I could feel his eyes on my neck as I resumed my journey through Tirmon.

The bull-nose Morris sat like a small, dogged animal at the far side of the village, a little wisp of white steam drifting from its bonnet. I ran the final fifty yards.

— Another minute and I was gone, said Tom King.

We lurched away, dust behind us.

— Is Frank all right?

— He's fine, Tom said and looked in his rear-view mirror. — Everything will be fine.

We drove for an hour, weaving back and forth through the lattice of tiny roads, gradually working south and then east, before meeting the main north–south road into Dublin. Tom had booked a cabin and two tickets in his own name on the mail boat to Holyhead that would sail that evening from Dún Laoghaire. Frank and Tom had spent the night before in the Dublin Mountains. Tom shook his head, as if trying to come to terms with the starkness and finality of the day. — These are queer old times, aren't they? he said.

— Did you hear that the Russians are heading for Berlin? I asked.

— It's a good omen, Tom said.

On the outskirts of Dublin, people were in their front gardens, digging or weeding.

— Can I ask you something? I said. — Why did Alice do what she did? She took months out of our lives. Why? If she hadn't, I'd never have agreed to marry another man, Frank and I would have gone away and by now we'd be free in England instead of being in danger here. Why did she do it?

Tom's big chin sank into his chest and he gripped the steering wheel. — It wasn't her, it was history. It was years of resentment and difference, it was people long dead whose blood is your blood. It was about wanting and having and greed. She saw her chance and she took it. With some people, it's beyond their control. She'd probably have liked you, you know.

— I can't understand it.

— You don't have to understand it, Tom said. — Frank tells me you have a sister much the same.

— Yes, I have, I said.

Old, bowler-hatted men sat on a canal bank in the sun, and beneath them, on the water, swans glided, their hinged reflections perfect. Trams veered around St Stephen's Green. Tom parked, nose in, and we walked together down Grafton Street. The billheads for the evening paper shouted, *WAR SOON OVER!* Metal wheels hummed on their tracks and bells clanged. Tom looked back over his shoulder more than once. We turned into Wicklow Street. I longed for Frank. Childbirth would be like this, I knew, pain bearable because of love. I went in through the Wicklow Hotel's revolving doors, and then through its homely hall, hat drawn over my eyes, past the panelled dining room with its white-jacketed waiters setting up for dinner, past the staircase up which we had gone together so often and so happily, and into the busy bar at the back. He was sitting in a booth near the door to the toilets, his face drawn and pale.

— I thought you'd never come.

I began to kiss him, not minding who was watching. I covered his face in kisses and he held me close and said, — It's all right.

I knew then, if ever I had been in doubt, that I loved him completely, for love, I understood, won't settle for anything less than its full entitlement. Tom handed him an envelope with the boat tickets.

— What time does she sail? Frank asked.

— Eight, said Tom.

— We don't want to go on board until the last minute, Frank said.

Tom went to the bar and I found myself checking the clock over the counter.

Frank asked, — What did you tell them at home?

— Nothing. They think I'll be there for supper, I said and had a sudden, guilty image of Mother sitting, waiting for me.

— That must have been difficult for you.

I looked at him and saw in his eyes what I had seen the first night.

— It's for the best, I said. — I'm just bringing forward what would have happened anyway.

Tom came back with whiskies and we swallowed them.

— I think we should get out to Dún Laoghaire, Tom said.
— The car is up on the Green.

— You two go first, Frank said. — I'll meet you at the car in five minutes.

I stood up and then, before I reached the door, looked back. The whiskey had brought some colour to his cheeks. He winked at me. I winked back. I went out the hall for the street, striding ahead, my chest filled with hope. And I saw Nick.

I turned, colliding with Tom.

— Tell Frank to get out! I hissed.

I faced the street again.

— Iz, what are you doing here? Nick asked.

— What do you mean? What are *you* doing? You're meant to be on a picnic.

— Iz, please …

I saw the two men: in long coats and slouch hats, they stood on the far side of the street by the windows of Switzers.

— Are you following me, Nick?

— Iz, I'm your brother-in-law, I care for you. So does Bella. We all care for you very much.

— So much so that you see fit to follow me.

— We know what's going on, Nick said. — Listen, please. This is not easy for either of us.

I could see the men glancing up and down the street.

Nick said, — None of this is your fault. But what is important is that you don't do something extremely stupid.

I looked defiantly at him. — I'll do exactly as I please, I said and reached back, for I knew Tom was now behind me, and linked my arm through his. — Come on, darling.

Nick's face was full of puzzlement.

— What are you looking at? Tom asked him and we walked arm in arm down Wicklow Street.

Every pair of eyes on the footpath of Grafton Street and from the trams seemed to be for us alone.

— Where is Frank? I whispered, walking fast, holding on to Tom as if to life.

— He got out through the toilets, Tom said, teeth gritted. — He's going to meet us in Dún Laoghaire.

I almost had to run to keep apace as we reached the top of Grafton Street.

— Get in, Tom said.

He went to the front, swung the handle and the old car shuddered to life in a cloud of soot. We reversed out and then lurched around the corner, up the Green, crossing the intersection into Harcourt Street at speed.

— Damn! Tom swore.

I looked behind. We were already halfway up Harcourt Street but at the bottom end I could see a big, boxy four-door saloon with prominent headlamps sway around the corner from the Green.

— What are we going to do?

— We're going to lead these fellas a right old spin, Tom said.

I could not bear to imagine that Mr Rafter had gone straight up to Longstead and alerted them to my behaviour, or that Nick and Bella would have me pursued like a thief rather than allow me my happiness; but for the past few months, I had lived in the realm of the unimaginable and this was little different. We crossed the canal bridge and came to fields of cattle. Tom forced the car to its maximum speed down a long, straight road. Little activity disturbed the village of Rathmines. We lurched through two bends, then climbed the tree-lined incline for Rathgar. The saloon was a confident fifty yards behind and, compared to us, moving easily.

— They may not know Frank was in the hotel, Tom said.
— They may think we still have to meet him.

We plunged downhill and along by the Dodder River. It was past four o'clock. Boys kicked a football at one end of a field in which cows were ambling home for milking. The dying sun still warmed one side of the street in the village of Rathfarnham. Church bells rang. I wondered what church we would marry in, and who would be there, or if the troubles – that persistent word that meant so much – would always mean our having to live somewhere other than in Ireland. In open country, the car began to slow against the foothills of the Dublin Mountains. Behind us, the saloon reduced its speed to match. Tom pulled out his watch. He said,

— The way I see it, the farther we drive, the longer the car behind will follow us and the safer it will be for Frank to catch the sailing.

— What do you mean?

— He's safe as long as they stay behind us.

— And what do I do?

Tom's big head was down. — You could join him later.

— How will I find him?

— He'll contact me like he did before.

We were now back on tiny winding roads barely wider than the car.

— Can't you go faster?

— I can try, but every five minutes we go is another five minutes to the boat.

The car groaned with every new mile. I didn't need to look back any more. I had something unique I could give him — his freedom. For by keeping on, by leading them after us, Frank would board the boat unharmed. I began to shake. I could not bear to think of losing him again.

— Damn it! Tom swore as thick steam began to rise from the car's stubby radiator. He threw the Morris around the next bend, and the one after, and the old chassis creaked. The road was potholed and the uncut hedges scraped its sides. Tom wrestled the wheel and the engine whined. On a straight stretch it appeared, for a moment, that we might have lost our pursuers, but then the saloon loomed into view, steadied, and with ease made up the difference it had lost. A steep downhill appeared. Tom aimed the car at the bottom without caution. The air was sucked from us as we dived. We'd reached the hill's base before the saloon had appeared at the top.

— Do you think we can shake them off?

— Are you religious? Tom asked, sweat on his face. — Because if you are, this would be a good time to say a prayer.

The radiator steam now made it difficult to see. A bend came up and we swung into it. Then another. The car seemed to career without purpose. I saw ditches head on, then road, then a bend so sharp there seemed no way out of it. We scraped through. An ass-cart appeared in the centre of the road as if dropped there from the sky. We veered madly, striking one of its shafts as we passed.

— Christ! Tom shouted.

The Morris slewed out of control, hitting both ditches.

I saw the cart, including its driver and the donkey, tilt over into the crown of the road. The Morris swerved on, sickeningly, then ploughed along the ditch and with a great bang, stopped.

— Tom?

Eels of blood wriggled down Tom's face. The braying of the upturned animal behind seemed to be the only sound. Then there was the roar of a powerful engine and brakes that screamed even louder than the ass. I looked back in time to see the saloon hit donkey and cart full square, spin once, then crash nose first into the stone pier of a gate.

I got out. Tom climbed out my side.

— Push, he said.

I got into the ditch behind the Morris, but I doubt that my efforts had any effect. I was aware that the saloon car now lacked most of its front section and that the donkey, feet to heaven, was dead. A man, the one who had been on the cart, lay inert in the ditch. Groans came from inside the saloon.

— Come on! Tom urged, red drops glistening on the tip of his chin and his nose.

I was ankle deep in muck. Tom got an inch on the back of the Morris, then another. Veins stood out massively at his temples. The car moved up, but then fell back and I sat down heavily.

— Come on!

I scrambled up and we pushed again. I felt possessed of strength beyond reason. All at once, the car sprang from the wet hole into which it had fallen. Tom dug deeper with his shoulder and kept pushing until the four wheels were on the hard road.

— God Almighty, I'm unfit, he panted. Then he went

around to the front. — Say that prayer now, he said and
swung the handle.

The car seemed to sigh, then shudder. He swung again
and nothing happened. I prayed: *Dear God, for my love.
Please.* Tom swung. There was a joyful explosion of life. Tom
looked back at the mayhem in the road.

— God save Ireland, he said.

It was dark as we made our way to Dún Laoghaire by way
of roads that had never known a signpost, over moors
where sheep roamed, their eyes yellow in the car's
headlights. I held Tom's watch in my hands. It was just past
seven. I willed the car on, but there was a speed beyond
which steam reappeared.

— These sailings are never on time, Tom kept saying.

— What will he do if I don't turn up?

— He has to go, Iz. It's too dangerous for him here.

I put my head down so that I would not have to witness
every new, agonising mile. We had somehow crossed the
mountains and were now chugging up the coast by the
seaside town of Bray. The car's engine coughed and
struggled and fine puffs of steam wafted inwards zephyr-
like beneath my feet. I caught sight of the dark bay which
our mail boat would soon cross, the grey-streaked night
water and the distant hump of Howth on the other side. It
was now half past seven.

— Oh, God!

A long vessel was putting out to sea.

— That's not her, Tom said.

— How do you know?

— That's a cargo ship.

I could not speak. I would die, I knew, if I were to see his ship on its way. Fresh sweat had broken out across the breadth of Tom's blood-streaked forehead and was causing the blood that had congealed there to drip anew.

— Don't worry, we'll make it, he said.

The road curved inland and the sea was lost. We passed through another village of dim streetlights. Abruptly, Tom swung right, down a narrow lane with house fronts on one side and a high wall on the other. Then the sea jumped out at us, the black vastness of it, and I could see the great, brooding outline of a ship at moorings and smoke rising from her single funnel.

— That's her, Tom grinned.

I wanted to throw my arms around his neck and tell him how I would never forget him, how he had risked so much not for some cause or spent idea, but just for his friend. He was straining now to see as we slowed down and drove along the grey wharf by the mail boat's stern.

— Where did he say he'd meet us?

— He didn't. But he'll have to be somewhere near the gangway. He's got your ticket, Tom said.

People were walking back to the quayside, many of them turning and waving up to passengers on deck. Lights flickered yellowly. The Morris jolted to a halt and we got out. The whole quayside reverberated to a massive blast from the mail boat's hooter. Then I saw him. He must have been standing in the shadow of heaped crates and boxes near the foot of the gangplank. I laughed. I wanted to tell him how incredible he was, how handsome, how beautiful I felt. I started to run. I laughed out loud. I wanted to tell him about the upturned ass-cart, about the wrecked saloon car of the stupid guards or whoever they had been, about

243

Nick's meanness and about how Tom was the best friend in the world. And he saw me laughing and he opened his mouth to tell me something, and he too was laughing, perhaps at the thought of how he'd squeezed out of the Wicklow, or maybe he was thinking of how this was just the first of many voyages that lay ahead of us, and how it had always been meant, from the very start, to work out for the best like this.

And then Tom screamed.

— *No! Frank! It's a trap!*

We were converging on the gangplank from both sides. I turned just as the boat's hooter erupted again and saw Tom's mouth open, but could hear nothing. And then we were alone, the three of us in the whole area, but not alone because all around us were men with outstretched arms, pointing, and I saw Tom catch himself with both hands at his chest and spin.

— Frank?

From far off I heard a man's shout.

— *Halt!*

Frank was ten yards from me. As he ran, he reached into the pocket of his jacket. I saw him gasp as the air was punched out of him, then heard the sharp snap of gunfire. His head went back and his body seemed to buck, as if trying to shrug off the attack, as if this was something he had often dealt with before. He fell, one leg twisted beneath him.

— *Frank!*

He looked asleep. He would open his eyes now and reach for my hand. I went to him. Blood thick on his lips. In his nostrils.

— *He's not dead!*

I fought them. My arms were held.

— *Frank!*

I screamed until one of them clamped his hand over my mouth. I bit him and he cursed and slapped me hard. I was glad he did that, but I would have preferred it if he'd shot me. I lunged at him and he hit me again.

— Take this mad bitch away.

As two big guards in uniform caught hold of me, I saw one of the plain clothes men squat down and gingerly catch Frank's wrist and pluck his hand from his jacket. The brown envelope with the tickets was between his fingers.

Chapter Eighteen

1945

On the first day of April, it began to rain before I got up, and when I did, eventually, the lawns of Longstead were mostly under an inch of water. Mother would be unable to set up out of doors. On the back landing beyond my bedroom, the strategic metal pail would prove its long-time use as the leak in some inaccessible gully reconfirmed its existence.

What had come to me out of the quivering emptiness of the intervening weeks was the silence. No one said anything. I could understand how Mother, who had her own grief to deal with, and the remaining staff at Longstead, who must have been fearful for the roof over their heads, would remain taciturn about an event that had made the front pages of the papers – two suspected subversives shot dead on the quay in Dún Laoghaire and the arrest and subsequent release of a Miss Ismay Seston in connection with the same incident – but the people I might have expected to comment never did. Neither Mr Rafter nor his son, John, when I encountered them, ever mentioned what everyone knew, but rather their eyes assumed an empty expression as if I were formless, someone on whom it was not possible to focus. The Misses Carr drove over in a trap pulled by matching bays and twittered around Mother for most of one afternoon, then clipped away at four p.m., having never allowed their eyes to rest on me for more than the briefest moment. Neither did Bella nor Nick in the days before their delayed departure speak to me about the events in Dún Laoghaire, nor of the murder of the man I loved and his friend; I was glad, for I did not wish to discuss it with them, but it still amazed me that they had not brought it up. No word came from Mount Penrose. That brought me no relief, for I knew Norman had been walking our acres and that he knew I was at home. Had he decided to be done with me he would, in Penrose fashion, have written, terminating our engagement and probably asking for the return of his mother's ring. In reality, he was biding his time, like a patient hunter waiting for the low point in his quarry's resistance before striking home. In a wider sense, I expected further visits from the guards, or army, or indeed from newspapers; there were none. It was as if something too shameful to address had taken place. Soon it would be as if it had all never happened.

I felt at first benumbed, then fearful, then almost nothing. I slept for days. I could see his face in every detail and clung to that image. I rarely went outside, staying upstairs in my room, sleeping. That was where I did my crying.

Time became shapeless. On freezing nights, I crawled to

the window like something fossilised and beheld the obscenely peeping stars. Weights dragged me down from where I wheeled in dizzy rings. In the ever folding darkness, my arms flapped and my shoulders stammered their helplessness. I could grasp nothing, just lay there, parched of mercy. Dawns came in atoms of blinding daylight that bore into my head. I reeled beneath the blur of awful colours and through my pounding blood saw the new day with its dull red rind. Cries of grief burst within me but were smothered as they floated upwards. Barely knowing, I skimmed the icy steppes of my memory for one extra moment of him. I craved that speck of time between his life and death so that I could ease myself into it and remain there forever. I began to wonder what had happened to the love we had shared, because we had kindled something beyond ourselves, a force too strong to be kept underground. I felt at times irrationally certain that what I had been through was a dream and that I would see his living face again.

The love I had known both buoyed and drowned me, for there were times when I knew I had lived rarely. We had been wonderful together. We had infused one another. I saw the silent people, and pitied them.

❧

A form arrived in late April from the Land Commission, requesting it be filled in and returned. A statement of the activities they knew did not exist on the acres they were poised to grab. I threw it to one side.

On the first day of May, as I got up from bed and saw the rain but did not care about it, and heard the dull drone of defeat, an awful nausea broke me out sweating all over and I stumbled to the enamel basin. I needed to lie down. I was drained and sick. Perhaps I was dying. Perhaps the flame we had kindled together was now going out and me with it. *Good*, I thought, and curled up and went to sleep. I ate nothing that day and was sick again that evening and the next morning. I could think then only of the financial burden of a long-term illness, of the length of time it had taken Daddy to die and of his final degradation.

The doctor who had come to Daddy lived in Trim; I went down to the village one day and asked John Rafter to drive me to him.

—You look well, Iz, he remarked.

It was all glib charity, I thought, no one could bear to face me with truth any more. John left me out in Trim; I went and sat for an hour before I was seen. The doctor's warm hands probed and pressed. He looked into my eyes.

—A little sample, if you wouldn't mind, Miss Seston, he said and handed me a kidney bowl before going discreetly behind a screen and turning on the taps of his wash hand basin.

He took the results of my performance and returned behind his screen. He came back out, a wry look on his face.

—You probably know already, he said.

— Know what?

He looked at me sceptically. — You're pregnant, Miss Seston.

John Rafter was waiting for me in the middle of the town.

— Are you all right, Iz? he asked, frowning.

I smiled. — I'm better now, thank you.

I made him drop me by our gates and walked up the avenue, feeling the wisdom of nature. Rooks flapped high in the trees and I was happy for them, for I was back at the beginning and time lay before me in abundance. As I neared the house, Mother waved to me from her place in the sun house. Inside, I sat at the desk in our rarely used drawing room, opened the middle drawer of it and took out a sheet of notepaper. I was both crying and laughing as I wrote, for I knew this would work. My words spilled across the page with fond purpose. The silent world would be outraged when it learned of my decision, but I did not care. There were worse outcomes than this, far worse. I signed the letter, put it in an envelope and addressed it to Ronnie Shaw, Esq., Sibrille, Monument.

EPILOGUE

The taxi made its way along Thomas Street, past the Guinness Brewery, then swung down by Christchurch and on to South Circular Road. Over Leeson Street Bridge and past the Burlington, it made the turn into Ballsbridge.

The pace of change bewildered Dick Coad. Even by the standards of a country solicitor, his understanding of global economics was limited, yet he deplored the daily erosion of history, the charge to transform by erasure. The house, on a quiet road near the embassy, came into view. It had changed little from the day he had come up with her in 1957. The same solidity, the same front garden, and back. The same chestnut tree – now *it* had changed, had grown, its leaves already yellowing in early September, reaching to the bay windows of the first floor where she had slept.

Dick paid the taxi, pushed in the gate and walked up the

path. He had been in love with her, he knew, but so too he was sure had every man who had ever met her.

— Good morning, Mr Coad.

— Miss Toms.

He followed her in and, by habit, sat in his usual chair before leaping up again.

— I'm sorry, I normally …

— Oh, sit, sit, said Bibs Toms, and I have Earl Grey ready because I know you and she always took it.

He watched her bring over the tray. She was still a big woman, although bent now and with much of the bulk gone from her.

— I don't know what to say, Bibs said, putting down the tea. — I never imagined this would happen. I don't deserve it.

— It is a wonderful outcome and one on which her heart was fixed, Dick said and savoured the fragrant tea. — You were very good to her.

— She was my friend.

—You nursed her. You allowed her to die here, at home.

— Oh, stop that. Now, you will have to advise me about leases and tenants and whatnot. Do you know, I'm nearly seventy-five and this will be the first time that I will ever have had money.

Dick flared alight a cigarette, then looked at her in fresh consternation, batting the smoke away with his hand. — I do apologise, I should have asked.

— *Pas de problème*, Bibs said and lit one herself. — Another bad habit she got me into. Smoked to the very end, you know.

— I'm glad, Dick said and they beheld each other with shining defiance.

He took out documents to do with probate and the transfer of property from his briefcase. Bibs signed for five minutes and Dick witnessed.

— Some fresh tea? she asked when they had finished.

Dick declined, looked at his watch. — I wonder if I might see the garden before I go?

Together they walked out the back and down the long garden of burgeoning plum and apple trees. The air was fragrant with summer's heat. The gardens of these houses extended all the way to a lane at the back; the properties either side had been chopped and mews houses built with entrances from the lane. Dick and Bibs came to a slated shed, an old apple house.

— Her pride, Bibs said and opened the door.

Dick peered into the dimness. On slatted shelves either side stood last year's apples, or what remained of them, each one to its space, separate from its neighbour. The smell was deep, almost like that of cider. All the boards of the roof sat snug and even. Although the space in here was small, it exuded a feeling of contentment.

— She spent most afternoons down here, Bibs said. — It was where she felt happiest.

— I may, you know, said Dick as they walked back, take some notes from the pages she left, purely for historical reasons, of course, because I'm sure she would not have wished that part of what she put down to be destroyed.

— Quite, Bibs said. — Of course.

— I mean, I don't think it would be going against the spirit of her instructions were I to jot down a few things, perhaps even copy some parts with a view to later expanding them. I'm quite used to this sort of thing. I've published a history of Monument, you know.

— Have you really? I didn't know.

— Oh yes. *A History of Monument and District.* You can buy it in the tourist office. In fact, you can buy it in the bookshop in WiseMart now.

— And did you write it under your own name? asked Bibs.

— Indeed I did. Richard Coad.

— I must remember that, said Bibs.

She walked with him to the front gate and stood there as he made his way to Ballsbridge to find a taxi. Nice man, but a dreadful squint. His father had hunted and she had kept his mare and brought it to the meets. Now his son was her solicitor. *Her solicitor!* Bibs giggled. The thought of it. She climbed the granite steps to the front door. The garden flat had a separate entrance and was let to people from the embassy for £600 a month. Bibs had gone weak when she had heard. She had not really believed it until today. £600 a month! She'd lived on a fraction of it all her life. Of course, some people might not know what to do with so much money, but Bibs did. Out near Bray was a woman with some land who took in stray horses. Dozens of the poor things, all shapes and sizes. Feed and bedding had to be purchased, vets bills had to be paid. Bibs had stood for hours outside freezing church gates with a collection box until her hands had all but fallen off. No need for that any more. She took the tea things to the kitchen sink and began to wash them, whistling.